That Old Familiar Pain: A Love Story Told In Memory

Edward D. Sandison

Published by RWG Publishing, 2019.

Table of Contents

That Old Familiar Pain
A Love Story Told In Memory
By Edward D. Sandison

Dedication

This book is dedicated with love
To an unrivaled artist
Dan Fogelberg
Rest in peace would've liked to have met you.

The Stage:

THE INCOMING CLASS OF 2014
CORDIALLY INVITES YOU
TO THE
25TH ANNIVERSARY
HIGH SCHOOL REUNION
PARTY
OF SAINT MARY MAGDALENE
BASILICA HIGH SCHOOL
CLASS OF 1988
IN THE SCHOOL GYMNASIUM
FRIDAY
AUGUST 2ND
AT 7:30 PM
The Class of 2014 Has Worked Hard To Make This One Special
So Think Twice Before You RSVP

Part One

Chapter One
July 31st, 2013

Russell James Blaudel crumpled up the invitation and tossed in the trash. "Just unpause The Duke." They looked at *Stagecoach*.

Monica Blaudel, his soon to be twenty year old daughter scrunched her brow. "John Wayne was meant to be a lonely ranger dad, you weren't."

Her dad was forty-three, about one seventy, five-nine, black hair graying at the temples and handsome. He sat on his favorite easy chair, a tannish affair that had been restored twice. Russ never intentionally threw anything away he loved—and despite his physical fitness routine, there was nothing better than sitting on his chair watching a classic with one of his twin children. No visible jewelry, no rings and thirteen years divorced.

"You've been on me about that since you were fifteen." His daughter was perched on the matching couch, jeans, old Brittany Spears T-shirt and bare feet tucked underneath her. She was every bit his daughter, though not as wiry, same black hair—except hers was halfway down her back in a straight pony tail. She wore her late mother's engagement ring on her right middle finger and her Confirmation crucifix was usually visible. She never wore boob shirts and her jeans were never too tight.

"I'm not unpausing *Stagecoach* until you talk about Kitty and Friday." Russ scratched a place above his clavicle. He couldn't remember the last time anyone in that house spoke Kitty's name. Appropriate, since his kids never met the woman.

Blaudel stretched in his suit pants, rolled up sleeves and loose tie. The top button of his white shirt was open and his pants were black. The living room size was medium and it was clean. He had grown up in this house, as had his kids. A million pictures of them, even some of them with his late ex-wife. The room was ordered. A few books; Chesterton, Lewis, Hahn, Sheen and Sheed as well as the family bible, he eyed the front door and the hall to the dining room as well as the stairs. There was an opposite hall to the kitchen. Behind the flat screen were sliding doors to the back yard. Finally, there was a den off the living room that had been the playroom for him and siblings, now the priest and nun;

then it was his kids' playroom and it had become his home office. "I have to wrap your present if you don't want to watch the movie."

"I do want to watch the movie and I'm old enough to not need presents, and we are going to discuss Friday," now the businessman sighed.

"Dinner at your favorite restaurant, dessert at the place of Rusty's choice, you bring Brett and he brings Lisa, a twentieth birthday to remember. Then I go home and let my grown kids fly." This had basically been the tradition since the kids had been kids, alternating restaurant and dessert choices.

"I changed the reservation 'till tomorrow and made sure your secretary's worked your schedule. Rusty and I discussed that reunion—this time you're going." Her father stood up.

"In twenty-five years I've never gone." He went to the window which made his daughter grimace. At that moment Rusty came down the stairs.

Rusty was every bit a junior, he looked practically identical to his dad at twenty. The younger wore jeans and sea green polo. Though he had inherited his mother's brown eyes, as his father and sister had blue—also the younger Blaudel wore glasses like his mother had and he wore her wedding band on his right pinky. "Movie over?"

"Paused," Russ explained, looking at the lawn.

"Did you tell him Kitty will be at this reunion?" Their father closed his eyes.

Chapter Two
August 2nd, 1980

Russell James Blaudel, ten years old, opened his eyes on the beautiful day in his backyard. "Tag, you're it." A hand touched his orange and red—ah, the seventies—striped turtleneck in the back. His too blue with white side striped shorts were something better left in the Carter administration. But hey!

"I'm on you." He turned, but his best friend was already running away. Pixie cut chestnut brown hair and a white T-shirt with yellow shorts, even at ten, Kathleen "Kitty" Slater was athletic. They both wore white sneakers and striped athletic socks.

Russ chased her around the oak tree. "Kit,"—he missed. "This is it Kitty, if I get you,"—he missed again.

"If you get me then what?" Squealing with glee, she evaded him again.

"I'll give you a new nickname," he grabbed the tomboy's shoulder just long enough and let go. They'd been playing in the backyard together so many years that neither remembered when the friendship began—probably in diapers.

Kitty went eye to eye with him. "Okay Russ, what is my new nickname?"

"No one can call you it but me," she took him by surprise by puckering up and quickly kissing him on the cheek. That was something new and it was their first kiss, puppy love.

He blushed and took a step back. "I'm gonna marry you someday." Strong words for a ten year old girl. But tell me that you've never heard it on a playground.

"Really?" She giggled again.

"Soooo... who am I?" From the living room window, his mother, Shana Marie Blaudel watched chuckling.

"You're my Kit Kat." They looked at each other smiling.

Kitty approached him "Kit Kat?" A cross between what everyone else called her and the actual name of her favorite candy bar.

"Mmmm... yeah."

"I like it." Dave Blaudel, the boy's father joined his mom and put his arm around her.

The elder Blaudel asked for an update and laughed.

Outside the conversation continued. "Good."

"But," he waited and then she tagged him and ran. "You're still it." Russ chased.

His parents laughed.

Chapter Three
2013

"I don't speak of her." Russ turned to his children and then walked to his office. "Turn the TV off and follow me." He opened the office door.

Monica got up and turned off the TV. She stopped the ancient VHS copy of *Stagecoach*. Then she and her brother padded after their father who turned the light on.

The office was different. It was not ordered. It had pictures of the kids, but it also had a birthday party picture from when Russ was fifteen, the only picture Rusty or his sister had ever seen, outside the yearbook, of Kitty Slater. There were also three framed movie posters; *The Searchers, The Rio Bravo and True Grit*. There were various papers, even wrapping paper and files around the corners of the room and the desk wasn't ordered. It was piled with a laptop as well as more papers and files.

"What dad?" his son asked.

Russ sat behind the desk. "We need a new topic and as this this is your last birthday on my watch." From the drawer he retrieved a box from Kay jewelers and an envelope.

"Daddy?" Monica asked. "I'll always be your little girl." She and her brother sat in the two folding chairs facing the desk.

Her father smiled. "Yes, you will. But," he sighed. "But you're not children anymore." He glanced at the picture of him and Kit Kat over his fifteenth birthday cake. Then he looked at Rusty fast. The twins noticed.

"You were twenty when she left dad," Monica ejaculated.

"I don't speak of it," was repeated. He but the velvety black box in front of her and the envelope in front of her brother.

"You don't have to face it as a lonely ranger," his daughter began.

"I don't remember you dating... ever, you and mom never went out. After the divorce, never, we had the same teachers you did," his son went on.

"You weren't like this with Kitty," they looked at each other, "and that ended,"—

"Twenty-three years ago Friday," Russ concluded.

"When you were twenty," Rusty concluded trying to be smart.

"That's why this birthday is such a big deal for you, dad. Your whole life hinges on when you were twenty," a new thought from the daughter.

"Childhood's end? Or something?" his son suggested, who looked his sister and they nodded. *Oy Vey*.

"Let me suggest something else." He got up and went to the window, opening the blinds and revealing the oak tree. "Maybe all your birthdays are precious to me because you two are precious to me and I watched twenty years go by in a blink."

Russ leaned against the window sill and looked at his kids. "And you feel that as over because you grew up at twenty?"

"That's the problem with you Monica, you're too damn smart." Though frustrated, her father beamed with pride.

"No dummies in Prelaw at Steubenville dad," Rusty joked.

"Or PreMed," she poked her brother.

"Yes, my life changed at twenty and I had to grow up." He sighed. "No, your mother and I weren't all I hoped for. But she gave me you two and I love you guys more than life itself."

"We love you too dad," they said together.

He went back his chair and held the back standing. "Kitty Slater is back and single, you gotta face her." This time it was Rusty.

"I agree Dad," Monica smiled.

Russ looked down and sighed. "Open your presents."

Chapter Four
1989

"Happy birthday Lover," Kitty, 19, told him and crossed her fine legs on his bed. Pink toenails, but everything else was tomboy. Toned and tan and she still had that beautiful pixie cut at 19. She was also perfect in her boyfriend's eyes. In those awkward years between becoming an adult and living as an adult a happy couple can really know joy.

Russ accepted the box. "What's this?" He was curious. He was hard to shop for. His dad had given up. The Business Major leaned against the wall with the poster of *The Searchers*.

"Open it," she said coyly. She looked around his room. Yes, he had grown up in it. College commuter—he was boring and she wouldn't have it any other way.

Except for the posters and the titles of his books the layout hasn't changed for her boyfriend in all the years they'd known each other. Friends and then older and then more than friends. Same twin bed, same crucifix, same dresser and he still had clothes on the floor.

"Okay." He tore the striped paper. "Oh my God."

Stagecoach on VHS.

In 1989 VHS was still expensive and not easy to buy classics. What do you get for the guy who has everything?

Something he just still may be using in twenty-four years.

"I guess you like it," she smiled.

"Like it," his eyes looked like saucers, "I,"—he looked up at Kitty's expectant face.

"Love it?" Her soft green eyes danced.

"Not as much as I love you Kit Kat," he kissed her. It was passionate and hard. They kissed beautifully and then Russ kissed down to her neck. Then they looked down and the VHS and he grinned. She put it on the nightstand and kissed him again. Then Kitty began to use her hands. It wasn't always the plan, but sometimes he gave in.

The jock and the egghead, two gorgeous college students very much in love, made love and when they were done, he held her tight. They spooned and she could tell he was happy but not completely at ease with the situation. This is why they made love so sporadically, he really was trying to wait for marriage.

"Are you going to Confession about this?" He would.

"Mmmm," he smelled her hair. "Let's think about something else." She was small but sturdy in his arms.

"Are you happy with me?" Stupid question.

"You're all I ever want Kit Kat." She kissed his arm.

"Even if I make you feel guilty sometimes?" she raised an eyebrow and studied Our Lord on the cross. She was also Catholic, but not as serious.

"Never said it was guilt. Never said I had any regrets. We can't get married in college, but we won't always be in college." Russ hesitated. "Holding you I feel... complete."

"You're the only person I let myself be a girl with." Raised by a single mother and a total Tomboy, Kitty was the Annie Oakley of Rose, CT.

"You are faster and stronger and a better shot than any man I know," he reminded her. "But to me, you're all woman."

"Oh, yeah?" she patted his arm and grinned. She had perfect little teeth.

"Tell me." Russ's heart was pounding in his chest, like love would make it explode.

"I beat Lieutenant Thompson in Target practice." He was the Reserves champion at the base she served at. Well, Kit Kat's boyfriend guessed she was now.

"That's amazing." Russ was never sure what she was saying when she talked military, but be never let on. "Kit Kat, that's really incredible," he leaned up and kissed her cheek. The room was very blue, the carpet very tan.

"I feel so empowered during drill," and they were the emptiest weekends of her boyfriend's life.

"I feel empowered when you smile." Kitty rolled over and her breasts pressed against her lover. "I feel more alive."

"You show me joy."

Chapter Five
2013

Rusty opened the envelope. "Oh, dad. The concert." Two rather expensive music tickets with backstage passes and two round trip train tickets. Also a dinner for two gift certificate at a famous restaurant. Not cheap.

"You and Lisa will enjoy yourselves. Take my Amex, if anything goes wrong," not like signing Russell Blaudel would be a lie.

"Thanks dad." Russ just grinned.

"My turn," Monica opened the box. It was a diamond bracelet with one charm, an M. She put it on. "Oh daddy." M for Monica. She had been named for her mother, but that woman had always been Mona, as long as anyone could remember. This young woman was Monica and always had been and always would be a Monica.

"Happy birthday." They got up and hugged their dad.

"Listen, dad,"—he cut them off.

"Did I ever tell you guys that you were and emergency C-section and your mom was out cold. I had to pick names on the spot and no I'm not creative." There was a forced chuckle at the often told anecdote.

"Dad!" His daughter sat on his lap and put an arm around him while his son leaned on the desk. "You've done the single dad thing amazingly for... well a lot longer than ten years. But we can stand on our own four feet," they grinned.

"Two twins equals two times two feet equals four feet." An old Blaudel family joke. Dad kept evading their queries.

Monica kept speaking. "You need to do what's right for you."

"And you guys think reconnecting with a woman who broke my heart twenty-three years ago is what's right for me?" Of course he was terrified.

"Yes," Monica kissed his cheek.

"Which one of you was born first again?" he was there, but he had always refused to tell them

They laughed and Rusty crossed his arms. "I always assumed it was her."

"You're both my mini mess." Monica had come out second, shhhh. "It's your turn to cook son, we're going to finish the movie."

"Not until you give us an answer," but she stood up.

"I'm going to be late for my face time with Father Tom if we don't move."
Father Tom Hudson was the rector of the Basillica of Saint Mary Magdelene,
Saint M's, and the businessman was the finance council chair, he also
volunteered almost everywhere else for the parish.

"All right," the twins stood.

"I'm going to pee, then I'll join you again," Monica promised.

"Pork chops ala Rusty," her brother went down the hall.

Their dad puts the tape back on, but was too wrapped up in who gave him
the copy.

Chapter Six
1989

Saint M's was not just a parish. Nor was it just the Cathedral Basilica that it housed. It was a sprawling neighborhood corner of Rose, CT. A forgotten to the World Depression era priest, whose life had been one of 'heroic virtue,' had spent a lifetime building Saint M's in honor of God through the intercession of Saint Mary Magdalene, the reformed prostitute. The church building was the largest in Connecticut. There was a K-8 school and a high school. There was both a boys and girls orphanage, low income apartments, single mother housing run by nuns and shelters run by monks or nuns and of course the state of the art hospital. All had the same motto, etched in stone: *caritas est maximus;* the greatest is charity.

The interior of the basilica itself had been untouched by the horror that was the nineteen-sixteen and seventies in Christian architecture. It was laid out like a gothic cathedral and painted in bright rococo frescoes with freezes. Except for the addition of *Novis Ordo* altar, it looked the same for a Latin Mass Congregant praying for his son World War II as for a single mom praying for her daughter deployed in Afghanistan. For that matter a businessman stopping in for a quick prayer before a meeting in 2013 would have seen the same church as had a nineteen year-old young woman stopping in for the Sacrament in 1989. It was testament to the fact that some things don't change or need to change.

What is not broken should not be fixed.

"Bless me Father for I have sinned." Kitty sat down in the Reconciliation Room facing Monsignor Max Drake. He recognized his old student.

"How are you Kathleen?" the young priest asked.

"Bad enough to be here," she frowned.

"How long has it been since your last Confession?" the presbyter asked.

"Um," She crossed her jean clad legs. "When was Confirmation?" She wore sneakers. Funny thing was if he remembered correctly, she wore the exact same demure tomboy outfit the day of her Confirmation, she never changed. A good priest, minister or rabbi knew his flock so he could help them.

He held a hand up. "I get it." Drake smiled, he had been there. "Welcome back."

"Right. I'm on Birth Control. I go to Mass sporadically and receive Communion. I curse and argue with my mom and I've made love to my boyfriend half a dozen times since we've been together—-well since we started three years ago."

The future bishop scratched his goatee. Kitty's friends called him 'Father What a shame.'

"Hmmm," he thought. "How old are you now?" He had an idea.

"Nineteen," is that all?

"How long have you been dating your young man?" That took her aback.

"Always." The college student smiled and her soft green eyes danced. "Russ and I have been Russ and me since we wore diapers," Drake smiled.

"How long do you want to be Russ and you?" What can be more important that? Why was he repeating himself? Could it be he was looking for an emotion behind her desire for Blaudel? A good loving emotion that would lead her to marriage?

"Forever." Her old hoody had a big M on it. He had the same hoody somewhere. It was the letter hoody of the high school attached to the basilica. He had taught more than a few classes there and coached varsity baseball one year. He had also played varsity baseball there, a long time ago. 'Doubles Drake,' the centerfielder.

Not unnoticed were the two words she had used, 'always and forever,' those were the words Father Drake used in every wedding homily and Monsignor Tomillo had put on the time capsule stone of the basilica.

"Are one or both of you thinking or trying to wait for marriage?" Fair question.

"He wants to. I just want to be with him." The priest waited. "Yes, marriage....sometime... erm.. someday..." she concluded after hesitation.

"But?" You can't shock a good priest.

"We're both still in college." A nod. "He wants to be able to support me when he gives me his name." Another nod. "His dad has an executive position waiting after college, he's been interning for five years, my egghead knows the job." The priest smiled. "It's just that Russ runs here every time we make love."

"You keep using that phrase." Drake leaned back and smoothed his purple stole.

"Making love?" Kitty shifted.

"Yes. What I'm hearing is that these are neither sought out lustful encounters or just about the physical." The Sacrament requires counseling. What she had confessed was still a sin, but 'why?' is the question historians and clergy and counselors should always ask.

"Um, I guess." She bit her lip. He'd give her absolution, but was delayed to help her stop being conflicted. His Confessor always reminded him 'leave the weight at Jesus' feet, *you* don't need to carry it.' Max tried very hard to impart that on his penitents.

"Do you love each other?" She had a weight on her shoulders.

"Very much?" he frowned. That was a question.

"Are you asking me or telling me?" the question mark concerned him.

"I'm telling you, very, very much." This time she was firm.

"Why?" Father Drake was looking up trying to remember his PreCana questions.

"Well..." she shrugged. "He makes me happy... and I guess I'm a better person because I know him... because he loves me." That's the right answer.

"Is he better?" And that is the sixty four million dollar question.

"Yes." She didn't even have to think. Drake smiled. He didn't know there was a letter waiting for him promoting him to bishop. He didn't care. Helping his flock would always come first.

The priest smiled. "That's the right answer."

"Good. But I need to be in the army reserves. It's part of how I define myself." She shifted again. It was a big Reconciliation Room. "It may take me away someday."

"I see." The presbyter thought for a moment. "Is... you said Russ... supportive?" Whether Russ had confessed to him or not, it was sacrosanct. A sacred trust.

Kitty did not have to hesitate. "Yes, yes he is."

"Then I think you two are right for each other and are making a gallant effort growing together but need to wait for marriage." That made her pause.

"'He takes church really serious, am I taking him away from God?" Drake shook his head.

"Has your young man ever expressed a desire to any vocation other than marriage?" That made Kitty laugh.

"You mean like priesthood?" The confessor nodded. "No."

"Didn't think so." There was a little table next to her and a stack of paperback Bibles. "Pick up a Bible please."

"Okay?" She put it on her lap.

"Genesis Chapter two verses twenty-two through twenty four." It took Kitty a minute to find the passage. She read.

"...and that is why man leaves the house of his father and mother and joins with his wife..." The passage goes own, but you've heard it.

Then she smiled. "Keep the Bible. Read it with him. Grow in Faith before God together."

"Okay." She closed it.

"You and mom okay?" Kitty hesitated. "You confessed,"—

"Oh yeah, made good." Drake nodded.

"Does Russ ask you to come to Mass with him?" She nodded. "I encourage you to come."

"Okay." She tried, but often he came alone.

"Okay," Drake sighed. "Now that other sin you confessed..."

Chapter Seven
2013

"Russ, you are a genius." Father Tom was Forty-three, an ex-Marine and very bright. He had a full salt and pepper beard to match his full head of salt and pepper hair. For that matter Russ's hair was doing well. The priest was solid. He always wore his priest suit, collar and all. He had not gained weight since he played football in Kitty's graduating class.

His office was a model of military efficiency. No paper, no book, no stole or holy water bottle out of place. They were going over the 2013-14 fiscal year parish budget and beyond all logic Russ had balanced the books and put some in the emergency fund. With declining attendance and a seventy year old roof the parish had been squeaking by for a while. Two years as finance chair—a volunteer position—and the businessman had balanced the budget twice. This was the first surplus in twenty years.

"Piece of cake." The linebacker laughed.

"Says the man who turned his dad's million dollar company into a hundred billion dollar company in fifteen years, while being a single parent," he put down his papers and picked up his Notre Dame mug—just soda. "Bishop, Drake is grateful." Yes, that Max Drake.

"Just numbers." Russ shrugged.

"I know for a fact you are a multi-millionaire, but live like you're making fifty or sixty grand." Again the businessman just shrugged.

"I don't take home that much." Only about four or five hundred grand a year. "The company absorbs a lot, we give away more than most but we're still raped in taxes." He sighed and looked at his soda. "All my employees and their families have excellent benefits,"—

"All on you." That was the worst kept secret in Rose County.

"All on Blaudel Inc. That was my dad's pledge, including retirement pensions. But I still have to pay the damn tax because I won't pay for abortions or artificial contraception." A shrug.

"But you pay for *everything* moral," the presbyter acknowledged.

"Yup."

"Commendable," the rector sipped his Arnold Palmer. "You and your kids?" Russ let that stew.

Blaudel pretended he was speaking of health insurance. "I am an employee—legally."

"Sure. So just between you and your confessor, what do you take home?" the businessman looked away. "Humor me." He told him and his old friend whistled. "Whoa."

"It's like this. I pay taxes. House taxes, car taxes, and then yard workers and staff and all the kids' education,"—he was evading.

"Of course." Tom kept trying to bring him back.

"Then I look at what's left in threes. Monica, Rusty and me. They don't know it, necessarily, but on third each is theirs. Some is their spending money, cars and cards and the rest is the trusts they don't know about until they finish school."

"So they learn." Responsibility.

"Yeah." Russ gave a winning grin.

"And yours?" He was a simple man.

"I save some. I drive a simple car and keep my old one as a spare. The rest, about thirty percent," he took a check from his suit coat. "Three months, made out to Saint M's, do with it as you see moral."

Father Tom picked it up.

That was a lot of zeroes. "Holy shit."

"Father!" What? You never heard clergy swear?

"Oh," the priest crossed himself. "Sorry Lord, but that's a lot."

"Feed the poor," was the soft response.

"I think the soup kitchen can find a use for this." Saint M's Soup Kitchen...

"Just keep it between us." The linebacker locked it in the middle drawer of his desk.

"Anonymous donation?" he smiled.

"Very biblical." There was some chuckling and then Hudson got up and pulled a card out from between two books. It was familiar.

He dropped the card from the high school reunion, their high school reunion on the table. "Shakespearean."

Russ went white. "To be or not be?"

"We all have to be something old friend." The priest quoted Father Leo's *Reflections* from EWTN. He finished his drink.

"I'm not going." He picked up the budget.

"She's going to be there." Tom Hudson had been their friend all through high school and he had been back from his two years in the marines to bring his drunk ass pal home from the bar the day she left. It had not been a pretty sight.

"That's why I'm not going." That elicited a sigh.

"Do you know when I decided to become a priest?" A knowing look came from over a bearded face.

That made Russ grin. "Prom night?" That was definitely *not* it. He had not been there. Hudson had been at boot camp already.

"Shut up." He laughed. "No, it was during my last football game across the street." The school and fields were across Basilica Way from the church building and rectory.

"What, did you see Jesus Christ in the end zone?" Anything to lighten the mood. Father Tom ignored him.

"Do you remember that the referee had a heart attack?" Sure, the story had been told. Kitty and her boyfriend had been at a movie.

"I read it in the paper." Or something.

"I watched Monsignor Drake vault his way onto the field and give Last Rights before the paramedics could get there and then practically forced his way into the ambulance to hold the stranger's hand as he lay dying."

"Those are the kind of things that earned him that MITRE." Monsignor Drake S.T.L, V.G. had become auxiliary bishop of Hartfield and then Bishop Maxwell Lawrence Drake of Rose.

"The point is that I had a moment of clarity. What was one football game in light of eternity?" Now that was a good point.

"So you rededicated your life?" Russ puts the budget down.

"No, I got off the fence." He smiled. "I had been torn up inside for years."

"Well, I'm glad. But you still went two years in the marines?" That seemed to be a contradiction. From the day after high school for one exact tour, he missed Desert Storm.

"To please my dad, he said give it two years. If I still wanted to be a father," the priest laughed. "He'd be my first confessee."

"You are a better priest." They laughed.

"Do you know that you're the most eligible bachelor in the parish?" the businessman stood up. He picked up his drink.

"Do you have something stronger?" The presbyter stood and stretched out his coat.

"I stopped drinking in the seminary." Hudson pushed back.

"Bishop, Drake? Father Flint? Father Shanahan?" They laughed. The bearded man motioned and walked to the door. "Anyone home?"

"Mac's upstairs." Father Mackenzie Flint, young priest.

The door was opened. "So?"

"Shit," he elongated the word. "He thinks you're a saint, you got him fooled."

Flint's parents, Mary Sue Mackenzie and Zak Flint were three years ahead of the rector in high school. Their son had been ordained less than a year. "You think he's got a beer?"

"He and the bishop are one beer a night guys." No harm in that if you're not an alcoholic.

There was a hallway with the obligatory pictures of the pope and Bishop—something that embarrassed Bishop Max immensely, but he was too humble to keep a separate residence. He slept in the smallest bedroom in the rectory. There was a beautiful painting of Saint John Paul II and a few Christian art prints. Like the whole rectory the walls were an oak panel.

The doors led to various offices, except the one at the far end of the hall. That one led to the private residence. Hudson fished his keys out of his pocket. "Here," Russ accepted the spare mug so the knob could be fiddled.

"Thanks." They passed through the living room. Somehow the clergy found a little more modern in the nineteen-thirties era, unchanged since built, living room. Then they found Father Mac barefoot in the kitchen in his black pants, white T-shirt and a Yankees robe.

The kitchen had been refurbished. It had the swinging door and a back door. Beyond that, it was just a kitchen with a good-sized table in the middle. It was stocked to feed four or five priests every day. The young ginger priest was reading the Lectionary, probably for Thursday morning's homily and sipping a plain white tea cup. "Father."

He looked up from over his glasses. "Mister Blaudel." He stood and held a hand out.

"Russ, please." They shook.

"Do you mind having a beer with our friend here?" the rector asked.

"Not at all," the parochial vicar went to the refrigerator. He knew his mentor didn't drink, so he brought two beers and an Arnold Palmer.

"Now, talk." Hudson opened his soda as he spoke.

"I'm done dating," Russ retorted. The younger priest looked at the older men feeling nervous. He wanted to leave.

"Look, you guys have a history,"—but he opened his beer.

"Stay boy," Father Tom ordered.

"I really don't want to discuss it with you either, Father." The businessman was annoyed.

"I'm not talking to you as your priest, I'm talking to you as a lifelong friend," Hudson corrected him.

"Fat chance," Blaudel did something he hadn't done in years; he swigged his beer.

"You think because I'm celibate, I don't know shit about love?" the rector asked. Russ just frowned and looked away. "I know that I always expected to celebrate you and Kitty's wedding. I know damn well that Mona never loved you, even though you were a model husband."

"I loved,"—whom could he say?

"I know all about once in lifetime loves. Heck, in four months as a priest Flint has buried a dozen octogenarians who left behind one. You and Kitty, that was perfect and that was true love." He sipped his drink and his protégé looked uncomfortable.

Russ looked at Hudson and sneered. "She left me. I moved on, and,"—but he was cut off. This was escalating. He had never moved on.

"You settled for second best," the rector barked. "Then you hid behind your 'patron saint of single dads' persona and tried to let yourself die inside."

"I cared for Mona very deeply," This was getting dicey.

"Maybe I should go," Flint started to get up.

"Maybe you should stay in reel me any when I get mean." The younger man felt like if that was his duty, he was a bit late.

Chapter Eight
1987

The sky was gray and beautiful. They sat on the hood of the Volkswagen facing the beach. They sang along to the radio, classic eighties.

Kitty was always one to play air drums and Russ couldn't sing to save his life. But they sang along when they were alone. They had a blanket on over the autumn night.

"Thank you, I needed this," she kissed him.

"You worked hard the last three weeks," she had studied and they had sat up all night with her mom and open textbooks so Kitty could learn enough geometry to get a B+.

You see, Kathleen Slater had to work for math and science. It wasn't that she was dumb, she was a brilliant girl, but we all have strengths and weaknesses. "I grind it out, but I learn."

"You put me to shame in politics and history." That made her laugh. "Don't get me started on PhysEd." He was a geek.

"I can think and I can fight, some girl," the chestnut pixie cut framed Kitty's ears elfishly.

"Debutantes and models don't have a monopoly on being female Kit Kat." Russ puts his arm around her.

The radio changed and he 'hoped (she) didn't mind that (her's) were the prettiest eyes he'd ever seen.'

"I'm never a girl unless we're alone. I'm always an alpha. I have to run situations and I have to be in control," he never felt the same way, but she scared many people. "Shit, I have trouble being on the bottom."

That made her boyfriend do something out of character, he raised an eyebrow. "You hit like Donnie Baseball, you play tennis like—shit I don't who won Wimbledon."

That cracked Kitty up. "Martina Navratilova."

"Right, except, you don't look like a man," she gave Russ a playful dead arm. "Ow, hey."

"Shhhh. Woose." They laughed.

"Under these sneakers my toes are pink, that's girly." He smiled. "Of course, you're the only one who sees them."

"And I'm grateful." His jacket was leather and his jeans blue. Her jeans were black her jacket, blue. They both wore gray sneakers.

"I'm not even a weakling when I'm here," Kitty whispered in Russ's ear. "But I'm vulnerable and sometimes..."

"On the beach?" He looked at the waves, reflecting the moonlight.

"In your arms." They smiled. "I can relax here, everywhere else I have my shields up."

"I'm at home in your arms," the egghead agreed. "You really like me!"

"Shut up Sally Field!" Kitty gave him another playful dead arm.

"Ow, Kit Kat." She laughed as he rubbed his arm.

"Woose."

She looked at the clouds, he looked at her eyes. "...so beautiful," she whispered.

"I agree, wholeheartedly."

Chapter Nine
2013

"Long before I was a priest I was your friend," Father Hudson went on. "I knew you guys inside and out."

"We have been friends a long time." Russ chuckled. "Hell, our high school bowling team has already produced the mayor, a judge of probate and the rector of the cathedral.

"And a living saint," Flint tipped his beer towards the businessman and elder two ignored the younger man's hero worship.

"You were better, both you and Kitty were better when you were together. You think she left because she thought you weren't good enough and you've been trying to prove yourself to the World since." Except he was good enough then he was too good for her now, as far as Hudson cared.

It's just that a Christian must look beyond petty things like 'good enough,' right? "Hey," Father Mac held up his hand. "This man,"—

"Grow up kid, no man is that perfect," Hudson barked. No, but he was a great one.

Russ stood, "fuck you Tom."

Flint was so shocked his chair slid back six inches. "Um," he was wondering why he wasn't upstairs... He didn't know the story.

"Yeah, well fuck you too." Father Tom slapped the table with his big marine sized paw, "I'm sorry you settled for second best and Mona was unfaithful, but that doesn't mean that you haven't been served up a second chance and are a damn moron fool for not taking advantage of it." Love is love. He straightened up. "All that was good in either of you was because of or in reaction to the other." He Crushed his half can—yeah, he was that strong—making a mess and tossed it, without looking, in the garbage can, nothing but net.

"I'm going home," Russ crumbled his beer can and flipped it to the garbage can.

"Air ball," Hudson forced a smile. Flint picked up the Lectionary nervously.

"Good night." Blaudel went out the back door of the rectory, the door slamming and around the corner to the side street walking past the convent toward his house. Even in loafers he felt lazy driving three blocks, so he reversed his route to go home.

He was alone for the moment. Just like that he had separated himself from a bright, cool house and found himself in a dimming beautiful hot summer night. He began to hum some Michael Bolton. Yes, damn it, he had been asking Kitty that, in his heart for twenty years and it pissed him off.

The empty night wasn't that empty.

Two nuns were out in front of the convent house in the evening twilight under the streetlamp. They were getting some work in before it got too late. One was sweeping the walk and one was raking the early leaves. They both wore simple habits and veils—but sneakers and they were both under forty. The dozen nuns that lived there were all under forty. They recognized him. "*Buenos tardes Senor* Blaudel," the older one, Sister Luz Agostino greeted.

"Hey Russ," Sister Leia Pond MSW greeted. They had become friends when he had helped her get on staff at the Saint M's hospital. She was a social worker. Oh, and yeah, her parents were Star Wars fanatics. Yes, she shrunk heads when she wasn't praying.

"Evening sisters," the father of twins mumbled and kept walking.

"Uh, -oh," the younger nun mumbled something to her friend in Spanish, there was a chink of her rake on the fence and click of the gate. The headshrinker chased the businessman down the road quietly. "Spill,"

"What?" he chuckled a bit.

"Something's bothering you," Russ didn't look at her and kept walking.

"What makes you say that?" the neighborhood was upper middle class and the kids on bikes were just starting to go in. A couple kids shot hoops. One dad played catch with his boy.

"Because they taught me in therapist school," the nun grinned.

"Well," the businessman stopped and sighed. "Do you think I settled for second best?"

Looking more like a teenager in a white habit rather than the qualified professional she was, Sister Leia looked up and thought for a moment, then back at him, "you're gonna need to give me more." The nun waited.

"I was in love with a woman as long as I could remember and she disappeared on August second, nineteen ninety," his voice cracked and he started walking.

"Did she die?" he followed.

"No," again the voice cracked, "she ran off to join the active duty military almost the exact minute that Iraq invaded Kuwait." She may not have been able to seem combat in Kuwait but it was just a matter of time.

"Whoa, I'm sorry." Pond patted his back.

"She never said goodbye." It was a surprise to see him wipe his eyes.

"Crap." There was a bench around the corner. "Sit, I'll give you a free session." A stranger wanted the story from the horse's mouth.

"Um," the businessman rubbed his clean-shaven face. "All right." He sat.

"How long after that was it before you started dating Mona?" She sat. She knew his kids through the parish and well widowers' stories are told, even if he is not technically a widower.

"I guess," he thought for a moment. "Thirteen months."

"Pretty fast to have twins that are twenty," a nod, "were you two ever happy?"

"I don't know, at five months pregnant, she moved into the guest room, then she wanted to be near the kids and even though I woke up with kids too..." a long exhale... "for five or six years more we slept in separate bedrooms. Then she moved out. Then she divorced me." Hey, Pond wouldn't repeat it, it was her job to be trustworthy.

"Were you cold or distant?" Russ closed his eyes and ran his hand between his knees. His tie hung between his legs and his head hung down as if in prayer.

"Sister,"—he was uncomfortable discussing his sex life with anyone. A celibate nun closer to his daughter's age than his, especially.

Sister Leia puts on her best German accent. "Just pretend I'm Doctor Freud, for I have heard it all before."

"For the brief time," he tried to open his eyes, but gave up and kept him closed pretending she was a fifty year old doctor, "Mona and I didn't make love as fulfilling as the few premarital times I did it with Kit Kat," he whispered.

"Kit Kat?" Pond asked.

"Colonel Kathleen Slater, well," a shrug as he straightened up, as if stronger. "Most people called her Kitty, but she was my Kit Kat."

"Were you a giving lover to Mona?" she waited for him get that. He blushed.

"To both of them," Russ looked past the nun, not wanting to look her in the eye. As a certified professional therapist, she took it all in stride.

"Was your lovemaking regular at the beginning of the marriage?" she asked. There was a long pause. "Yes."

"Did she know about Kitty?" Now he did look at sister Leia.

"From day one there were no secrets about our pasts. I'm not a man to ask or care how many men there were before my wife committed to me," he waited for approval.

"As a therapist, I am inclined to agree," Pond touched his shoulder. "Go on."

"Kit Kat was just an ex who broke my heart." Russ shrugged again. "No one thought she'd come back. We all have at least one ex like her."

"Really?" came the Freudian response.

"Sorry sister," the businessman was embarrassed.

"Yeah, you're funny." Pond threw back her head and cracked up. Her ice-blue eyes danced. "The big JC wasn't my first boyfriend." That finally made Russ remember how to laugh. "I had my heart broken and broke a few hearts in high school," this floored her patient, "but Jesus will be my *last* husband."

"Good for you." The headshrinker came back over her face.

"So what happened in the rectory that made you so angry?" There it was.

"Well, Father Tom wants me to go to the high school reunion Friday because Kit Kat will be there." Sister Leia waited. "I don't want to see her."

"Sounds like she's more than a story in your past," Pond concluded. "She seems to be more like your own personal ghost that goes with you everywhere." Leia was right. Blaudel could almost see Kit Kat in her battle fatigues, right in the corner of his eye, but it was just his memory playing tricks. There was a long silence.

The therapist went blurry. "Wipe your eyes."

The businessman straightened up. "How so?"

"I... oh shit. I love my kids... don't think I don't love my kids,"—the expert cut him off.

"This isn't about your kids," she corrected.

"Excuse me?" Russ retorted.

"No, this is about you. Your model fatherhood is separate from your love for Kitty or Mona. I'd have less patients if more children were like yours and understood that divorce and or marriage is between husband and wife and is not about the kids—even if it harms them." That was not exactly what he understood to be Catholic teaching and he told her as much. "First of all I'm speaking as a therapist and not a nun. Second of all Mother Church teaches that a marriage must be open to children, not because of pre-existing children. The fracturing of a marriage is not between dad and the kids or mom and the kids rather between husband and wife and the children should never blame themselves."

"Rusty and Monica never blamed themselves," he agree.

"No, they never did, nor will they blame Kitty, she didn't will their parents to divorce..." This nun knew her brains as well as her rosaries.

"You're speaking in the future tense,"—why was everyone!

"Yes, I am, my professional opinion is that you need to face her."

Chapter Ten
August 2nd, 1986

"Summer breeze, makes me feel fine, blowing through the jasmine in mind," Kitty sang and at her pauses her boyfriend whistled the music.

She and Russ were hiking in the State Park a mile from Rose in Cannonville. Both the city of Rose and the town of Cannonville were on I-95 in southwestern Connecticut. A beautiful hilly park region with great views and set paths with posted maps as well as 'rest benches.' It was a beautiful day to be walking outside.

"Your baby sister would love this." The dusty earth, bounced up as they walked. Russ wore the Timberlands he had been given the Christmas before, jeans and a green sweat-soaked polo.

Kitty wore her old Adidas sneakers, which led past white socks to suntanned tone legs to light athletic shorts and a tied off white T-shirt, also sweat-soaked. On days like this bras were visible; not that her boyfriend minded. "Yes, yes, she would." The athlete took her beloved's hand. They walked humming some more Seals and Kroft.

"Oh, look, there's a map." It wasn't much bigger than a street sign. "We can turn left to the river, right back to the bathrooms or straight on the rustic shelter, whatever that is." The egghead traced the lines.

"Let's expand our horizons and find out what a rustic shelter is," that made him kiss her.

"What a genius you are." Not that they both hadn't had the same idea.

Young love is sweet and simple, even if the changes in their bodies are complicated. They were sixteen, too young to have the Hamlet Problem, but too old to call it puppy love. They didn't worry about the future and were too young to have regrets.

Kitty could hit a softball three hundred feet, out swim any opponent, get to any tennis ball and outrun any man she knew. She had a canon from right field and could steal bases. Don't get me started on her soccer skills. Russ could do none of that, but she taught him to run and he could keep up with her hiking with very little difficulty.

What mattered that day was that they were doing nothing at all immoral and enjoying each other's company immensely. The World was big and they didn't need to think about it. Kitty just held her young man's hand and smiled. She was at peace. Still strong and yet vulnerable—this was her most human.

Being vulnerable is not being weak. Christ was vulnerable on Calvary. Scarlet O'Hara refused to be vulnerable. Julius Caesar was never vulnerable. Rhett's ex-wife and Rome's ex *Imperator* met such great ends. Princess Leia was always vulnerable with Han Solo and tough as nails and more butt-kicking than anyone with everyone else. Queen Victoria was just 'your wife' to Prince Albert but Empress of India with everyone else. Should I go on? This is a fact that the future soldier would never forget. She would impart that on as many friends as possible. In her whole life she only let one man in though, only one person saw the real her.

She knew that for her young man the numbers added up when he was with her. They passed another marker and began to playfully count their steps.

"That's it?" A simple old bench, two posts, a slanted wooden roof with a piece of aluminum siding. Kitty sounded dejected.

"Oh, Kit Kat," Russ put his arm around her. "It could be worse." There was a thunderclap and off in the distance, maybe some lighting.

"It's worse," they looked and the sky. "Run," they took each other's hand and ran for the rustic shelter. "Damn," her hair was already wet.

"So much for 'light sun showers,' channel eight." His girlfriend didn't get mad. As they huddled under the lean-to, arms around each other getting soaked by the short burst of rain they laughed out loud. When it lightened up she spoke.

"I'm cold." The rain started to lighten. He was colder.

"Race you to the car," she looked at him shivering. Hair matted, water dripping down her face. She raised an eyebrow.

Then she gave him a fast closed mouth kiss, "I'll beat you," and the slippery athlete was off before Russ knew what hit him.

"Kit Kat!" he ran after her. The sight of her toned and tanned legs getting muddy was always ahead of her boyfriend the half mile back to their car.

His girlfriend reached her Volkswagen first. She had turned sixteen first and was a better driver. They didn't tell their parents that he had put a lot of money into that automobile.

The car was running, the heater on and the passenger door open and waiting. Russ jumped in and closed the door. Kitty tossed half the blanket from the back seat over her boyfriend. There was bedlam around the panting teens. Dozens of hikers were rushing for cover and jumping into cars. The Volkswagen was full of laughter. The radio was on.

"...what could make me feel this way—my girl..." Russ sang off key and Kitty gave him a playful dead arm.

"Ow, Kit Kat," she put a finger to his lips.

"Shhh. Woose."

Chapter Eleven
2013

"I have been a single father since my twins were very young, I mean Mona was absent plenty before that," Russ spoke evasively.

"Was she unfaithful?" The therapist asked.

"Almost from day one." Pond frowned. He raised a hand. "They're my kids, even if the visual evidence isn't enough, my lawyer required it for the divorce, though... heh," it wasn't a happy chuckle, "Sally—my attorney, didn't believe they were mine..." a fake smile... "they are." The nun chuckled.

"Oh come one, she looks like you in a wig and if you put on a pair of glasses you'd be him." Everyone said that about Monica and Rusty

"Yeah.". That made Blaudel smile.

"So Mona was unfaithful sexually while you were as faithful as any man can be—despite being in love with another woman." That made Russ look aghast. He opened his mouth to protest indignantly, but thought the better of it and closed it. "I'm neither condoning Mona nor condemning you. But you have to ask yourself have you ever and if you so, whenever did you stop loving Kitty."

"I," he wiped at his eyes with his handkerchief. "I have to think about that one."

Sister Leia nodded. "Where is Mona now?" she asked.

"Saint M's cemetery," her 'patient,' blurted out matter-of-factly.

"Oh, I'm sorry." Now she knew for sure. The animate therapist folded her hands in her lap.

"She passed away of breast cancer three years after the divorce." Considering Pond was in college at the time there was no expectation that she'd know that.

"Oh my, did she reconcile with the kids?" Russ puts his handkerchief away.

"Don't worry, we were all there." He stood up.

"Whoa, sit down sailor." The therapist pulled on the businessman's arm. "Articulate."

"Well," he sat.

Chapter Twelve
December 25th, 1986

Christmas party at the Blaudels. Maggie, Russ's older sister and Augie, her twin, the seminarian were there. As were both of their parents and Kitty's mom; Sharon Slater. The adults were in the kitchen with a bottle of telling stories of decades the kids couldn't remember. Kitty had gone to the ladies room,

"Kit Kat, he's on." They'd grown up with this song. Every December. Every damn December. She rushed into the living room as Russ turned the radio dial up:

Met my old lover in the grocery store. The snow was falling Christmas Eve, I stood behind her in the frozen foods. And I touched her on the sleeve.

She didn't recognize the face at first but then her eyes flew open wide. She went to hug me and she spilled her purse. And we laughed until we cried.

We took her groceries to the checkout stand. The food was totaled up and bagged. We stood there lost in our embarrassment. As the conversation lagged.

We went to have ourselves a drink or two. But couldn't find an open bar. We bought a six-pack at the liquor store and we drank it in her car.

We drank a toast to innocence. We drank a toast to now. We tried to reach beyond the emptiness But neither one knew how.

She said she's married her an architect who kept her warm and safe and dry. She would have liked to say she loved the man But she didn't like to lie.

I said the years had been a friend to her and that her eyes were still as blue. But in those eyes I wasn't sure if I saw. Doubt or gratitude.

She said she saw me in the record stores and that I must be doing well. I said the audience was heavenly But the traveling was Hell.

We drank a toast to innocence. We drank a toast to now. We tried to reach beyond the emptiness But neither one knew how.

We drank a toast to innocence. We drank a toast to time. Reliving, in our eloquence. Another "Auld Lang Syne".

The beer was empty and our tongues were tired and running out of things to say. She gave a kiss to me as I got out and I watched her drive away.

Just for a moment I was back at school and felt that old familiar pain, as I turned to make my way back home. The snow turned into rain.

"What a bitch," was Kitty's deep response. She nuzzled her boyfriend on the coach.

"Why is she a—witch?" Maggie, who rarely cursed, asked. She sat in one chair and Augie was in a folding chair, turning down the volume. He wore a black sweater over white turtleneck, black trousers and black shoes, almost priestly already.

"She broke Dan Fogelberg's heart." That was what the athlete who looked out of place in a long skirt, flats and garish Christmas sweater her mom had bought her thought.

"That's all you get from the song?" Russ asked.

"No, it's about second chances happening too late. It's about realizing you can't go back again," the elder brother suggested. "Kind of a downer, but he understood you need to let go of the past and keep moving forward, everyone has to grow up eventually."

"Why can't you go home again?" his brother's girlfriend asked.

"Maybe you can?" Magdalene Marie Blaudel suggested. She wore a conservative long floral dress and had her legs crossed demurely.

"That would be nice," her younger brother suggested as someone sang Jingle Bells and he kissed his girlfriend.

"What does it mean, 'the snow turned into rain,' Lover?" Kitty asked.

"Maybe, winter's over Kitty?" Augustine Louis Blaudel offered.

"The cold and dead past... the ghosts... are gone and spring is here Kit Kat?" Russell James Blaudel suggested.

"So where he's going, that is better?" the pixie cut beauty asked.

"Possibly," the seminarian suggested.

"But he definitely said home and you just said you can't go home again," the younger woman suggested.

"It's a figure of speech, Kitty," Maggie corrected. "Home is where you hang your hat." The woman who'd spend most of the next quarter century in a cloistered convent suggested.

Jose wanted to wish them a merry Christmas on the radio in Spanish. "Or where your heart is," Russ countered.

"So, as the poet says, you're"—her boyfriend's lips cut her off.

"Agreed."

"You guys are too much." The older brother sipped his egg nog. "I heard an interview with the esteemed mister Fogelberg. He says this is a real event in his life."

"I like green eye's better Kit Kat," Russ spoke up and she put a finger to his lips playfully. As opposed to 'as blue'.

"Go on Augie." He cleared his throat.

"He is in a relationship in real life, so 'going home,' refers to his girlfriend, or wife and family. Perhaps he knows his life is better now than it could ever be with her."

"Then why does watching her leave cause him pain?" the athlete pressed.

"It is a love song." Russ looked out the window at the lack of snow.

"Maybe someday my little brother will be in slushy snow watching you drive away," his sister suggested, half-jokingly. If she only knew

"I won't drive drunk I promise," he retorted playfully. That elicited a playful dead arm. "Ow, Kit Kat." Thank God for Tom Hudson.

"Shhh. Woose." She kissed him. "Why would you ever have to watch me leave?"

Chapter Thirteen
August 1st, 2013

Monica was grilling chicken for lunch with her brother. When one or both twins were home, they took turns on meals with their father on a cycle. They were old enough to cook, he had taught them well and they actually liked it. They also shared in the vacuuming and mopping. Russ hadn't done their laundry in years.

Rusty padded in in sweatpants and a stinky Lady Gaga T-shirt. He had jogged that early afternoon. He had a band behind his glasses to hold them on around his head. "Hey sis." Unlike most twenty year-old siblings, they actually enjoyed each other's company.

Monica was also barefoot. Black toenails that matched black jeans and she had on a pretty purple top that had a high neckline. Her hair was in her signature ponytail. "Chicken's almost ready." He opened the fridge and got the orange juice.

"Juice?" he asked.

"Please." Her brother got two glasses and poured.

The kitchen had been done by their mom right before she moved out with granite counters and an oak breakfast table to match oak cabinets. The expenditure had been so much that their father hadn't redone it since.

Rusty left the half gallon on the table and sat, gulping his juice. Then he looked at the window and frowned. "Were we too hard on dad last night?

Monica flipped the chickens. "What makes you say that?"

"I got up to get some milk last night and he was in his office, I peeked and he had scotch and a yearbook." That was a rare sight. They had never seen either parent intoxicated and that yearbook gathered dust.

The daughter didn't turn because she faced the vegetables in the frying pan. "Was he listening to Chicago?" *Oh boy.*

Her brother thought. "Oh shit," then he rethought. "Which one is Chicago?" She told him. "No, it wasn't."

"Who was it?" She stirred the veggies.

"Oh, I don't know that old shit," they laughed at each other. They had grown up on that stuff and she still listened to it.

"What did you hear?" She turned the burner off, the silverware was spread out and there were always napkins piled in the middle of the four person table.

"Something about 'she married herself an architect,' it sounded almost Christmassy."

"Shit," his sister spread the contents of the frying pan on two plates that were on the stove. "That's a great song about lost love that he always avoids." She turned all burners off.

"Well," her brother refilled his juice. "He wasn't avoiding it last night."

Monica moved the chicken to the plates. "Yes, we were too hard on him."

"Oh boy," it was somber. The bespectacled future doctor watched the frying pan get put in the sink and full of water before he got his food.

"I just wanted to see daddy happy," the future lawyer argued as she put the plates down.

Rusty looked at the food and crossed himself, a simple grace his dad had taught him. His sister followed. "This isn't over. Mom didn't want to see him miserable, that's why she left." Mom was also sick of being miserable.

"You know, there's only two good things about that union." They looked at each other.

"I'm glad you're here too sis," the clinked glasses.

"Mom didn't love daddy, she pitied him," Monica almost sounded like she was in court.

"That's a bit..." her brother used cutting his meat to think of a word, "harsh."

"You lived here too, you saw everything I did. We may have only been that young when she died, but I saw what was happening between them." The future lawyer picked up a bite and then put the fork down. "You saw what he did when she was too sick and too alone."

"After that doofus Bobby Joe left?" Finally, she took a bite. So did he. "Delicious."

"Thank you." They thought for a moment. "Mom was friendless, penniless and without family. She had a couple painful months to live. No one owed her anything. She was all alone."

Rusty finished another bite. "So dad went and picked her up at hospice. He paid all the bills and brought her a hospital bed here."

"Don't forget the nurses," Monica rubbed her clear nails on her left hand, then her right; against her sleeves, her nervous habit.

"She asked him 'Why?' That's it, just one word." They looked at the rings on their right hands. He rolled his. That's the question, isn't it?

"It's okay Mona. Be comfortable. See your kids."

"It's creepy how well we know that dialogue and can do their voices." Monica laughed at that. "But seriously, he was free and clear of his ex-wife and still he took her in and gave her the best care as possible when she was sick with cancer."

"Who does that?" Rusty was at a loss.

"Dad apparently, the Saint of Rose, Connecticut," that had drained their appetites.

"She was always talking to him odd when she was sick." His sister thought about that one. "She looked at him weird."

"Like he was dying or dead inside?" They sat with that and tried to eat, but they suddenly weren't hungry.

"Do you know how many of my friends came from broken homes?" the brother asked.

"Half of mine," his sister put her utensils down, giving up.

"Mine too," the wiry future doctor sighed.

"It sucks," she sipped her juice.

"Don't ever say that phrase in court counselor," Monica rolled her eyes and they laughed.

"It still sucks." They weren't bantering. Brother and sister were having an adult conversation.

"Do you know many... hell any that lived with their dads?" Rusty asked.

The sister scrunched her brow. She had broken more than a few hearts already. "Few of my friends had or have any kind of relationships with their dads." She looked at the linoleum floor, a white, blue pattern of squares, it was unclear what she was feeling.

"But we did and he was amazing." The brother's words seemed to perk his sister up.

"I'm not questioning his fatherhood; I'm saying it takes two to destroy a marriage." She got up and went to the open window by the sink. "Maybe mom wasn't the only one at fault in that marriage."

"You said it yourself, we lived in this house, we may not have been in that marriage, but we were close enough to see what she did to him." Monica lit a cigarette, took a drag and blew it out the window. Size ten, little makeup, demure and beautiful but she did smoke. Nobody's perfect. Her brother was handsome like her dad, or at least all her friends said so.

"I'm not defending or condoning mom in any way Rusty, I'm just saying it couldn't have been easy for a woman to live in a marriage where it wasn't just her and her husband, but also the ghost of a woman he really loved." The future doctor watched the cigarette smoke go out the window somberly.

"You don't have enough information to convict him of that counselor," the brother begged to differ. Yes, she did.

"Oh really," the sister crushed out her cigarette and tossed it out the window. "Exhibit A. Refusal to attend any high school reunions and exhibit B. a failed marriage."

"Objection, your honor, circumstantial," They had been playing this game since she caught the 'I want to be an attorney' bug while watching *Law and Order*, and they played it about just about anything they disagreed on.

"Exhibit C." She produced a half empty bottle of scotch from the cabinet. "Exhibit D. Witness testimony to *Same Auld Syne.*"

"Again, circumstantial," Rusty got up to get the plastic wrap from the drawer.

"I submit to you the many examples, on record of how he avoids the topic," wrapping the plates in plastic wrap her brother shook his head.

"Nah." Hardly court talk.

"And finally I submit me," the future lawyer did a little twirl.

"You?" her brother chuckled.

"He raised me to be the anti-Kitty. Demure, a bookworm, more conservative clothing, no sports—not that I minded." A chuckle. She took the plates and buried them in the refrigerator. "As if he wanted to make sure I never do to a man what she did to him."

"You have a problem there counselor," he countered.

"I do?" His sister puts the plastic wrap away. Then she sat opposite her opponent and they crossed their legs.

"We have never met Miss Kathleen Slater. Other than a few references in a dusty old yearbook, you have nothing on her personality." He leaned back and crossed his arms. The future doctor grinned.

"Oh really," his sister stretched out the syllables and, knowing the tone her brother stopped grinning. "Eighth grade Catechism? Who was your teacher and who was mine?" That question was not an easy answer.

"Shit, it was a long time ago. I remember we had been split up that year." He scratched his clean shaven face.

"Honestly, I forgot yours, but mine was Miss Slater." Monica crossed her arms and put her feet up, leaning back. "Nice woman."

"I take it that was Kitty's mom." She nodded. "And you have kept up a friendship?"

"She's a nice woman, pushing seventy now, finally married. Her daughter made lieutenant colonel a ways back and Sharon's a very proud mom." So the challenger waited. "A lot of folks about town went to school with dad," Monica cackled, "the mayor, Father Tom, Docror Bueno... I have a knack for getting information." She giggled.

"Does the prosecution rest?" Rusty was down.

"Sure." she sipped her juice.

"When mom was sick and dad took her in, what was that?" That was a fair question.

Monica puts her feet down and then her hands to her nose for a moment. "Hmmm." She looked up to the side. "Herbert Kappler."

"You better help me on that one." The sister crossed her legs and the brother picked up the orange juice to put away.

"I'd bet money he's in Heaven, but he was a repentant monster." That just confused her sibling more, who closed the refrigerator and put his arms out; palms up. "Kappler was the Nazi who ran all of Rome except the Vatican during the Occupation."

"And?"

"He killed Allies, Jews, priests and anyone else that pissed him off." It was once a famous story. "One Jesuit stood against him, Monsignor O'Flaherty. This ballsy Vatican pencil pusher saved thousands of lives while running an underground network."

"Sounds like the plo

t of one of those old time movies that you watched with dad." His sister smiled, blue eyes dancing.

"They did dramatize it for TV, but that's not the point. The Nazis fell and Kappler was arrested and sentenced to life imprisonment and O'Flaherty served the Church fifteen more years. No one came to see the Nazi,"—

"Why would they?"

"Why would the man who denied Jesus three times be named Saint Peter and why was the man who killed Saint Stephen chosen to be Saint Paul?" Rusty took his glasses off and rubbed his eyes.

"You're hurting my head counselor." She patted his shoulder.

"To be a Christian is to forgive. Once a month for much more than a decade the Monsignor visited Kappler in prison and finally received him into the Church." The future doctor replaced his glasses. He was stunned.

"Still spinning." History wasn't his subject.

"Someone had to be kind to him and forgive. Mom needed someone. Dad is so Catholic that he knows how to forgive. He may not trust, but he forgives well." They stood up. "In kind, she forgave him." Trust?

"Is that it, he's afraid he can't trust her? Or all women?" he took the empty glasses to the sink. "Is that why he doesn't date?"

"I don't know Rusty. I think I would like Kitty if I knew her. But when she left him she fucked him up real good. She did everything but make him gay."

"But we can't condemn him," he put his hand to his sister's shoulder.

"Of course not. You don't forget a love like that. You try to find it again," She stretched. "I don't hold any of this against him."

Chapter Fourteen
1990

"Checkmate," Russ moved a pawn.

"A pawn a goddamn pawn!" they sat at the old Blaudel dining room table and played chess over diet Cokes.

"Look at the board Kit Kat," she had wanted to play for real, it wasn't his fault. He gave her time. She didn't have an old Yale educated maternal grandfather that taught her all of the ins and out of that black and white board.

"I," she reached for her king, as if to tip it with her left hand, but it was a ploy, she gave her boyfriend a playful dead arm. He reached for the pain.

"Ow—come on,"—she put a finger to his lips.

"Shhh. Woose." Kitty was laughing at Russ. He didn't mind. Funny thing was he liked the dead arms and he really liked watching her eyes when she laughed.

"Another game?" he asked with a sly grin.

"No," she laughed. "Get the poker chips." She dumped the chess pieces in the box.

"All right, but mom's upstairs Kit Kat," she put a finger to his lips.

"I didn't say strip poker," now her boyfriend laughed.

Sometimes life together was just fun.

Part Two

Chapter One
August 1st, 2013

Colonel Meghan Rose Brewster was having a very good day. Not only was she months from being the youngest female general in U.S history, but she had her least favorite Lieutenant Colonel's discharge papers on her desk. Brewster was career military and a combat veteran. She was married to an army doctor; they met when he sewed her up once, just a broken leg and a small scar.

'Colonel Meg,' was an officer's officer. Respected by those below her and above her on the food chain; gender didn't matter in her rise or the way she served or to whom she served with. Men looked up to her. She had won a medal of honor dragging a man out of a building in Baghdad, while under heavy fire and with a broken leg and took out an entire enemy cell—single handedly—while holding her position.

She loved being a soldier, but had one thorn in her side since she her early days as lieutenant. Lieutenant Colonel Kathleen Slater. "I'm not going to miss you, you bitch." There was a knock on the door. Could something interrupt such pleasure?

"Enter." Lieutenant Victor Gump, her tall, dark and four-eyed aid entered.

"General Olson is here." If Brewster was a proper soldier, trouser and creases with red hair in a bun, then Lianna Olson was her opposite. She had never seen combat and spent most of her career in requisitions. She was blonde, wore the skirted dress uniform and let her hair down as soft as regs allowed. But she was close to retirement.

"Show her in." The colonel stood.

"Very well," the aide disappeared and entered the general. Brewster stood and saluted. The general responded half-heartedly.

"Have a seat." She waited for Gump to close the door and then the older woman sat as well. No one could prove it, but the scuttlebutt was that the General dyed her hair, she was in her fifties. Meg was... younger.

"Did you call her?" the higher rank smoothed her skirt.

"Was almost ready, I'm relishing it. Good riddance. "She picked up the papers."

"Good, it's that attitude that is why I haven't told her yet." Olson's stars glinted.

"You didn't." Meg dropped the papers, "Ma'am." She bit her lip. "She doesn't know that she retiring as a full colonel?" *Shit.*

"On the one hand she will never be functionally the same rank as you because her discharge is official today, but on the other hand," the general's voice got harder, "unfortunately because everyone knows that despite your one great moment she was twice the soldier you are."

"Excuse me General?" the colonel tried to keep her cool.

"How many combat injuries have you sustained Meg?" Olson asked.

"Ma'am?" she knew Olson had none. "If I may,"—

"I know I have none but I'm much older than you and I never have pretended my service to this nation was half of Kitty's." Blonde hair and hard blue eyes.

"I was only injured the once." She gestured to her Medal of,—

"Why did you join the service Colonel Brewster?" General Olson asked.

"I wanted to make,"—but the older woman was on a roll.

"Don't give me the script. You followed in the footsteps of your father, the General, your grandfather the colonel, your grandmother the army nurse and both great grandfathers, wounded enlisted men in combat, am I close?" *Smug bitch, ain't you?*

"All right General, what's your point?" A shrug followed.

"You got where you are based on one act of inhuman bravery and fifteen years of ass kissing Meg," a fiery redhead stood.

"Generally, you are treading very close to harassment." She started to reach for the intercom to get a witness.

"Shut up junior, my pension's secure." The finger stopped moving.

"This will be your last chance to talk to Colonel Slater. She never kissed ass, she once told off a general—spitting in his eye for endangering her men. That type of attitude saved a lot of men's life, I bet they're not sorry she's a bitch. Kitty fought bravely for this country since she was twenty years old winning several purple hearts and more medals than the two of us in this room put together." Olson smoothed her blouse coat.

"Ma'am," Brewster stood at attention, "I am not aware of a new army policy that rewards insubordination." She was seething.

"I suppose," the general inspected her nails, "MacArthur, Patton and Eisenhower made a living keeping their mouths shut? Julius Caesar was content to farm next to the Rubicon and Napoleon was happy in Egypt?"

"Are you comparing that... that, former officer to a president and two emperors?" the colonel asked rudely.

"No, but there was a time a great officer was an outspoken hot head. If I had to lead an invasion of Normandy or crouch in a foxhole I'd sure like to have a dozen or so insolent bitches just like her on either side of me," she crossed her arms.

Brewster grimaced. "Really?"

"You were freaking lucky that day, weren't you?" Meg sat.

"Is this about me?" she asked.

"No, it's about a soldier that has been held back by this army, mostly by other women for being too much of a bitch." That was true.

"General, may I speak freely?" She'd love to talk about how Slater had left a trail of emotional wreckage in the men she'd taken for lovers, scuttlebutt said her sex life was mercenary and she was incapable of commitment.

"Is it about her personal life?" The superior officer knew.

"Yes, ma'am," now the colonel was nervous.

"No. I've heard plenty of rumors, it's irrelevant." That made steam come out of her subordinate's ears. "You know what's relevant?"

"What?" Meg began to chew on the inside of her mouth, to avoid talking back. That's how her career moved forward. She'd learned that from her father, who never talked back.

"She's a soldier's soldier." that's very different than being an officer's officer. "Have you read her file?" a shake of the angry head. "Especially since the last time she was injured, I decided to get to know her. So I read it. Do you know when she enlisted in the army?"

"I," she paused and then shrugged.

"She joined the ROTC and the Reserves as soon as she was eligible. She drilled every weekend, never missed one, until August second, nineteen ninety." The colonel glazed over. "August second, nineteen ninety." Just blank. "You can't be that young."

"What am I missing?" Brewster asked.

"She transferred her commission from the Reserves to active duty army the day Iraq invaded Kuwait, even though the ban on women in combat hadn't yet and worked her ass off to earn an appointment to West Point and then to where she is now..." as she spoke Lianna wondered what Kitty Slater was thinking about on her way home to Connecticut.

Chapter Two
August 2nd, 1984

Russ and Kitty were walking. "Tell me more about ROTC." They held hands and ignored the passing cars and the children on bicycles and skateboards. It was the middle of the afternoon on a beautiful summer in Rose. They dressed like soon to be ninth graders, one preppy and one sporty dressed. His hair was perfect facsimile of Michael J. Fox's and hers was her traditional pixie cut.

"It's something to do," she gave him an impish grin. "No it's about college."

"College?" he laughed. "We don't start high school until September second." The impish grin deepened and those beautiful soft green eyes danced.

"Four years of ROTC gives me four years of some college scholarship money." Too polite to talk about it, but even at fourteen the egghead intuited that Sharon Slater, though she worked hard, wasn't a wealthy parent. But what she didn't have in the bank she made up in love.

"A ride to college, that would be worth an after school program Kit Kat," he swung her hand playfully. It also looked good on the application.

"It's more than a few afternoons and less than all of college according to mom. But there are other colleges, scholarships and..." she shrugged.

"Really?" Don't expect a fourteen year-old to fathom the cost of college; or of student loans. Hell, without the GI Bill, athletics or Russ' parents no one would get a free ride.

"So, what college?" he was in a rush, Russ wanted to go into business with his dad. Blaudel Inc. was a diverse manufacturing, import-export Company. He had already decided on a hard workload at URose and internships.

"I dunno, that's like four years away dude," she giggled and gave him a fake dead arm.

"Ow, Kitty"—

"Shhhh. Woose."

"Oh come on." They laughed.

"What are we doing tonight?" she asked her boyfriend.

"Well, mom cooked a large ham. Maggie's eating dinner with us before some church thing. Then I thought we could watch a movie," he answered his girlfriend.

"Ugh, not another John Wayne movie," Kitty rolled her eyes and he almost tripped over his feet while getting lost in her eyes.

"You picked that Arnold Stallone movie last week," he argued with a grin. So, he loved The Duke, as early as he could remember his mom watched *Rio Bravo*, *El Dorado*, *McClintock* and *Stagecoach* with him.

She stopped walking for a minute she was laughing so hard. "Arnold Stallone?" he shrugged and put his hands out, palms up.

"I'm not into these big budget R-rated movies," she laughed at him. Of course she was surprised his mom let him watch them. "Come on." Russ blushed.

"Does the little girl want watch a Jane Austen movie?" his girlfriend spoke in a faux mocking voice. She giggled, first Russ was angry, then her eyes calmed him. They always had that effect on him.

Kit Kat's soft green eyes. They were a world all in themselves. Well, two worlds. As long as he could remember Russ remembered that those eyes could always calm him. They always spoke to his soul. Whether as kids and she won a fight. As adolescents, when the World was so confusing she brought him peace. As a young adult first tasting real love...

"Just my luck, I date the only girl who likes big guns, bigger explosions and the once in a while boobie." She giggled and started walking again, he started after her.

"You don't like boobies?" He glanced at the places he could not touch just for a moment and then back to her face. Ah the sweet pains of adolescence.

"Of course I,"—she gave him dead arm playfully. "Hey, Come on,"—

"Shhh, Woose." She loved making him uncomfortable.

"I'll race you to the oak tree." She meant the one behind his house.

"All,"—she was already off. "Kit Kat!"

"Woose." Russ ran after his athletic gal for the three turns and a block and a half. She used her hands and jumped his parents' short metal fence, he stopped and opened the gate. They couldn't be sure, they were too wrapped up in each other to really pay attention, but at least two cars beeped at them as they crossed streets.

"Kit Kat!" he called panting as she put both hands on the big tree with great shade.

"I got you!" She always got him. Her boyfriend fell against the tree, sweat soaked and exhausted. His arm was bent and he used it between the bark and his head as a pillow.

"It's okay my woose," his girlfriend chided. "I'll be running miles twelve weekends a year in the ROTC." That made him sad. Time without her. It wasn't that he was possessive, just...attached.

"My God, you're a tough chick." She pecked him on the forehead. "Thanks Kit Kat."

"Didn't John Wayne play a soldier a few times?" Russ smiled.

"Yeah," a broader grin, "he even was up for an Oscar for one, pilgrim." They laughed out loud.

Chapter Three
2013

Colonel Meg Brewster sat in her office alone. Her very good day was not very good now. She looked at the phone. Then at the papers and then back at the phone, grimacing. "If I make four star general, it won't make up for this." Finally, the pissed off officer picked up the phone and dialed.

"Slater," Kitty's voice came full of static. *Damn cell phones.*

"You can answer hello and go by Kitty again, your discharge is complete, honorably," the woman behind the desk spoke coldly.

"Colonel Brewster," the retired officer responded colder.

"Is the ride home from the VA satisfactory?" It had better be, they were putting too many resources into this woman for Meg's sanity as it was.

"I don't know," there was muffled talking, "what do you think Bob? Is my chariot sufficient?" Then there was the muffled sound of laughter, as she seemed to flirt with her driver. *Shameless.* "It works."

"I have been ordered to congratulate you Kitty," Brewster went on full of disgust.

"What for?" yes, the retiree was being catty, but she and Meg hated each other. They were like two teenage girls after the same boy.

"When you get to the residence that Uncle Sam secured for you, near the VA in Rose, Connecticut, you will find another package from General Olson," This was a hard damn phone call. Oh, Brewster was not happy.

"Flowers? Wine? Good scotch?" this was some muffled talking and laughing and then she came back speaking sarcastically, "condoms? Cuban cigars."

"You're eagles, colonel. You have been officially discharged with the rank of full colonel with all of the privileges and responsibilities a retired officer of that rank has earned," the words felt like razor blades coming out of the younger woman's mouth.

"Wow, that must have been hard for you to say Meg." Brewster opened her mouth to argue and then closed it. "We're the same rank again, I'll call you Meg, Meg." The phone was almost slammed down. "Meg, Meg, Meg."

"Kitty,"—but she was cut off.

"Meg, Meg, Meg, Meg. Me-eg." The last one the syllable was stretched out. Bob, the driver's laughter could be heard.

"Kitty. *Kitty!*" Was the barked response.

"Oh, come on Meg, don't you realize that 'well-behaved women never make history,' right Bobby?" There was more muffled talking and laughter. "Bobby says yes."

"Come on now, when were you ever a feminist Slater?" the still on the books officer barked into the phone, disgusted.

"Feminism? I don't need feminism. Feminism needs me. Women who just succeed on their own like Margaret Thatcher give feminism a bad name because we don't need it. That's why feminists hate us." Now it was more like a cackle.

"I can't talk to you. But that's okay. After this, we never have to talk again." This was all true and Brewster couldn't wait.

"Oh come on, it's over. I won't miss your by the book hardass attitude," what had started out as a good day had become a *frigan' shitty day*.

"The VA is prepared for you, you have an appointment Monday, oh nine hundred..." she rattled off some data... "and as you requested your mother has the keys and will meet you at the apartment..." The few boxes and footlocker of gear from Kitty's last apartment was sent ahead as well. They could avoid each other from now on and Meg's nemesis could go back to her pre-army life and...

Chapter Four
August 2nd, 1988

"Are you ready?" Kitty asked, her arm around her boyfriend watching *Back to School* on his parents' couch.

"For URose?" It was the second largest public university in Connecticut and while it didn't have the reputation of Yale it was more respectable.

"I think so," that was one thing she loved about him, he was humble. Of course he was ready. He had fifteen advanced placement credits and finished eleventh in in their graduating class, yet he never talked about, all she could talk about was her. "What about you Kit Kat?"

"RCTC?" (Rose Community Technical College), "why wouldn't I be ready?" his girlfriend had chosen a different path. She was going to go part time and work full time. He was going to go full time and interning at his dad's company.

Sure, Blaudel Inc. was one of the reasons that he chose to commute, but everyone knew that Russ wanted to be in Rose for Kitty. His parents didn't mind. One sibling was a Jesuit and one was in a convent in Quebec. They were ecstatic to have a son close—even more so in entering the family business. Not to mention the fact that Kitty was already a member of the family as far as Blaudels were concerned. "Is it what you want?"

"I'm with you, I'll get going and there's always a PE teacher certificate someday," her boyfriend was unconvinced. He was not worried yet. He figured that he'd be making enough after college to support her, little did he know how much more he'd be making, but he didn't care. Silver and gold were just things. Kitty was his treasure.

They chuckled at the movie. "You could always be a bouncer." She twisted away and gave him a playful dead arm. "Ow, Kit Kat."

"Shhh. Woose." More laughter and dancing eyes and they went back to watching TV.

They couldn't have been more content.

Chapter Five
2013

Sharon Slater-Burns was the polar opposite, physically, of her daughter. She hyphenated her name because getting married for the first time at sixtyish meant that she was known by her old name too well, she also liked being a Slater. She was a beautiful woman in her youth, though never scrawny. She hovered around a size 22 most of her life. She had given her chestnut hair and soft green eyes to her daughter. Of course the mother's hair had gone gray before sixty—some time.

She had bypassed Rose Mall and Trumbull Mall for Milford Mall. The hour drive was worth it to go to that mecca of New England shopping right off I-95. Sure, there had been visits had various posts—including Hawaii—in twenty-three years, but her little girl was coming home and the Slater-Burns account could afford the two grand in housewarming gifts this proud mama had bought.

She had just merged her immaculate blue Dodge Stratus onto I-95 South when her phone rang. She pressed speaker, recognizing the number. "Hello Kitty."

"Ugh, mom, that drove me crazy at ten," but the forty-three year-old was giggling.

"Listen kid, you'll always be my Hello Kitty," funny thing was that her tomboy daughter *never* liked that damn cartoon feline.

"Thanks ma, we're in Jersey now, shouldn't be an hour, Bobby says there's no traffic this time of day." Sharon switched to the middle lane.

"Oooh, Bobby?" There was some muffled laughing.

"Sergeant Robert Gunderson of the motor pool, he was ordered to drive me home." *Now wasn't that nice of the frigan army that stole my daughter's youth.*

"Do you need anything?" she asked.

"There is a nice apartment waiting for me, a pension, all my gear has been delivered and a nice therapist at the VA ready to start discussing PTSD on Monday." *Right, PTSD, That's all.* Not all of the mother's worst fears had not come true but therapist and PTSD and VA were not words she ever wanted to hear.

"Kitty, listen." Somebody beeped their horn and Slater-Burns had to accelerate. "Are you alright, I mean,"—

"I know what you mean mom," her daughter sighed. "I even got promoted my last day in the army." That really didn't help, but like all good parents, she knew how to fake it.

"Wow, that is... that's awesome." It almost sounded genuine.

"How's Bill?" being military she didn't know her stepfather well, but William Burns had met Sharon Slater at work when both were fifty-eight and he was divorced with grown kids as well and he made Sharon happy and that was all Kitty cared about.

"He's..." yeah, they were that new... "wonderful."

"He's your favorite subject ma," the daughter quipped with an audible grin. Traffic forced the mother back into the right lane.

"*You* are my favorite subject Kitty." Yes, she was lapping it on a bit thick.

"I was glad I could make the wedding in Boston," Bill was from Quincy, Mass, a suburb and he had too many invitees not to placate them. He had moved to Cannonville on business long before and had had a messy divorce. His children were in their thirties. There were two boys whose names escaped the colonel and Patty, a rather likable Irish daughter of thirty-eight. She and her husband, apparently also lived in Cannonville. After the wedding, the house that Kitty had grown up was sold and Bill sold his house and they bought a condo.

"You know that Russ Blaudel bought us a couple grand worth of silverware, both for everyday use and special occasions." She had to say that name. It wasn't clear, but it sounded like the younger woman started to pant.

"That was nice of him, why didn't he show... guess he forgot," it wasn't supposed to, but it came out like a hiss. "Bet he didn't RSVP."

"Actually, he RSVPed in person. We sat over tea and talked for hours." That made, the older woman smile. "Always loved that kid and he turned out to be one amazing man."

"And you never thought to bring this up?" Kitty was dejected. Sharon wanted to get under her skin, it was working. Now if she could get Russ and her daughter to admit it. Maybe if she got them together...maybe at the reunion and they had to talk?

"Why does it matter?" There was a long pregnant pause.

"It doesn't. Why... er... I wouldn't care if he was there or not?" Of course her voice cracked. Mama knows how much her child does care.

"What would have you done if had been there?" Nothing. "What if he had asked you to dance?" There was a long pause. "Kitty, Bing Crosby said that 'the only thing more obvious than two people looking longingly at each other is two people trying desperately to avoid it,' I think you two have done everything possible to avoid looking at each other since the day you left."

"That's crazy mom." That was a point for the mother.

"Oh, yeah? So why'd you freak about him missing my wedding?" Nothing. "I could have seen you two dancing the night away."

"Not funny on so many levels," the daughter was annoyed. "Mom, Russ was wonderful, but he... but he...he is in my past." The past? Why did her voice crack. She could almost see him, her own ghost, out of the corner of her eye in his business suit. Just her memory playing tricks on her. Two points for mom.

"You left him without one complaint on his character," She just disappeared in one day. "You never said what he did." Mom knew. Moms always know.

"Because he never did anything wrong!" Kitty rushed to the defense of her former lover. "He was wonderful, but I had to be a soldier...it is part of me." There was a hesitation. "The service was in me and being in the service was me."

"You could serve and be with him," now they were just butting heads. The trees lining the interstate were beautiful.

"He would have had to leave Rose and give up his business dreams!" Now the daughter was just angry. Another point for mom.

"You two were you two from the time you were in diapers, in those two decades, was that really the most important thing in his life?" That made her take time and think. Sharon looked at the radio "Here this may jog your memory *not that different* by Colin Raye."

"Ma," her mother did this a lot —Sharon sang along a bit. "First of all, life is not a Collin Raye song and second of all I was neither seeking someone more exotic or greener pastures." Game set match.

"So you admit Russ is perfect. Or at least perfect for you?" Oh Sharon was on a roll now.

"Of course he *was.* Twenty-three years ago. I'm sure his wife would disagree," she knew better than that and her mother told her so. She sounded more like she was trying to convince herself.

"She's very long gone. He's completely free." Slater-Burns was polite and left out the part about how that it was a marriage of straw.

"That shipped sailed ma," there was muffled laugh. Apparently it had sounded like naval humor to sergeant what's his name. "I've...lived..."

"I don't care about your sex life daughter, you're a grown woman,"—Sharon began.

"A middle aged woman now, mother," there was muffled speaking. "Shush Bob."

"But when was the last time that you were in love?" *I should have been a lawyer,* Slater-Burns thought to herself. She knew the answer already.

There was some hemming and hawing, "Well, I did share an apartment,"—

"Did you ever say to that nice captain, "I love you?" that led to a long pause. Finally, very soberly her daughter said one quiet syllable. "No."

"Your twenty-fifth high school reunion is tomorrow and Patty and I both think you should go,"—there it was.

"Is Patty involved?" there had never been cattiness or any hostilities between the stepsisters. Hell, they had both pressured their lonely sixtyish parents to marry. "Really? She never met Russ Blaudel,"—or so Kitty assumed.

"Now that you're coming home, I had hoped you two could be friends," Sharon had begun to the think of herself as a grandmother to Patty's kids and they thought of her has third grandmother. So it's more like two daughters getting closer.

"She's met Monica Blaudel and they get along great, in fact Monica's babysat the grandkids a few times, great kid," the grimace and sigh was audible over the phone.

"See, he has a great daughter. I bet his son is great too. He has a family. That's not something you just walk into and disrupt." There was the sound of a forty-three year-old fist hitting a car door.

"He's divorced. His ex-wife is long dead and his kids are both twenty, they're grown." Nothing. "He's the most eligible bachelor at my church."

"See," Sharon felt herself losing this one.

"He lives like a monk." That was her last card to play.

"Ooops, there's a tunnel mom, I got to go,"—

"To the reunion," hey, it was worth a try.

"No, have to hang,"—click.

"Shit."

Chapter Six
August 2nd, 1989

It was a raucous party at a friend's dorm. There were half a dozen students of both genders on either side cheering either Russ or Kitty on. Yes, there was underage drinking—it's college. No one was driving. They were on opposite sides of a ping Pong table, he had two Solo cups left and she had three. Make that he had one—his girlfriend bounced a ball right into one of his. "Beirut!" the other teens yelled.

"All right," slowly, painfully, Russ drank the beer in the cup, rolled the ball into his hand and flipped the cup onto the upside down pile. "My turn," he leaned back.

As you've guessed they were playing Beer Pong. The variable where the ½ cups of beer are arranged like bowling pins on either side. The goal is to bounce the ball into one of the opponent's cups. If you succeed, they drink. First one out of cups loses. "Bring it on."

Her boyfriend eyed her front cup and closed one eye and bounced the ball over the net, over the cups and onto the floor. "Miss!" the spectators yelled.

"My turn," Kitty picked up the ball and didn't bother aiming. In two bounces she sunk it. "Beirut!"

"Beirut!" the spectators echoed.

"Damn." Russ drank and then flipped the cup over on the ball.

"I'm out," his girlfriend picked up her diet Coke.

"Me too," her boyfriend walked around the table. Two other coeds took their places and reset the board.

"No making out with the loser," one of them ordered.

"Right," Kitty tipped her drink mockingly and took Russ's hand. "I need Oxygen," her smiling egghead nodded.

"Come on Kit Kat." The dorm rec room was on the ground floor near an exit to mini park—just two benches and a couple trees.

"I want to beat you," one girl called.

"Maybe later," again the diet Coke was tipped as they walked away. Hand in hand, they walked to the bench. Russ and Kitty sat down. "Ugh!"

"You okay Kit Kat?" he started to put his arm around her.

"Cramps," he reached for her belly and rubbed it. "Damn fool, shouldn't have drank." But she knew this would work.

"There, there." She started to feel better, "you kicked my ass." She forced a giggled.

"That's right." She kissed him. "Oh, that makes me feel better," he rubbed her tight belly above the waist and it made her relax.

"At least we know you're not pregnant Kitty," she giggled.

"I don't know how I could be, knowing you." He kissed her forehead.

"Just feel better." The happy eyes had an odd look.

"What did I do to deserve you?" She studied his face.

Russ smiled. "You're just my Kit Kat."

Kitty didn't have to respond. She just smiled, beautiful soft green eyes dancing.

That was pretty damn good night. They shared a million memories like that.

Chapter Seven
2013

Patricia Marie "Patty" Scolari Nee Burns didn't know her step sister Kitty Slater well, but she liked her and hoped now that she was coming home they could be friends. She sat in her simple suburban living room, kids at school—the hours of a soccer mom's delight in her loose sweatpants with oversized Yankees T-shirt and turned the TV off. She had long blonde hair and freckles, dark green eyes and shopped in the size sixteen to eighteen range.

"It's worth a try." There was a Post-it note on her phone with a ten digit phone number.

"Slat—hello," still getting used to civilian life, apparently.

"Kitty?" there was a pause and a groan.

"Patty?" an affirmative was murmured. "I'm never sorry to hear from you, but if mom put you up to this,"—

"Actually, it was the young woman who babysat my kids last night." There was a long pause. "Her name is,"—

"Monica Blaudel." The veteran spoke very flatly.

"Yes."

"Bet she has black hair, blue eyes and looks just like her dad." Good guess. Patty spoke sarcasm as a second language.

"You gonna be a psychic?" That made Kitty laugh. "She's great with kids, terrible at sports but does have a long black pony that she does use to block when they shoot hoops. Unfortunately, she can't make a shot."

"Sounds like a debutante. A real Heartbreaker," You have to understand, twenty-three years in the military Russ's ex-lover spent demonizing the woman he married. So she assumed Mona was like that and the kids took after Mona.

"Not at all. Monica is the sweetest girl. She and her young man go to Mass together every Sunday. Their talking marriage, they're going to the same law school." There was a very long drawn out silence. "Are you still there?"

"Yeah, I'm sorry. What's her brother like?" *Well, at least she's interested.*

"He runs. He never competed though. He and Monica played Maria and Riff in *West Side Story* in high school. He also plays the piano with a surgeon's precision, which is probably why he's preMed. He and his gal seem tight."

"No athletics for either one of them?" the veteran's tone had turned inquisitor.

"Nah. Rusty looks just like Russ, 'cept for the eyes. He has his mother's eyes and wears glasses. As far as all the women at the Basilica say, those two men could share pants. Mr. Blaudel has the same waistline, *he* had at twenty."

"So what?" *Oooh. I know your reputation. That impresses you.*

"Why don't you want to see him?" Patty didn't have the whole story and she was curious." What puts a wedge between two people that were never known to fight?

"Patty, I,—Bob just pulled into the Stamford Rest Area... no I'm fine... yes go." There was some mumbling and the sound of a door. "Good, he has to pee." Her turn to try to make sense of it to an outsider.

"Just us girls?" They giggled. *Just us girls and the NSA are listening in.* Why would the NSA care anyway?

"Sure. Why not?" There was a long sigh. "Do you love Tony?"

"My husband?" There was a murmur of assent. "Of course."

"Tell me about that. Feeling? Action? Sex?" That gave her pause.

"I guess I like me better with him than I like myself alone or with anyone else, much better." That was fair. It wasn't the security. Patty was a published journalist, she could support herself. Her answer was from the heart.

"And him?" Good point.

Mrs. Scolari thought for a moment and then chuckled. "Tony skipped a softball championship because I had bad morning sickness with our first child. He stayed home and took care of me and cost himself a trophy. He said that 'he was only a winner when he was with me anyway.' That has been his attitude for the almost fifteen years since we met."

"Okay. I get it, because that's how I felt with Russ Blaudel and that's how he felt with me. Even when I lost championship games... you know." The voice on the other end of the line cracked.

Patty spoke from ignorance and without speaking, "how do you walk away from someone like that... from a love like,"—

"I don't know, I just know I did. Twenty-three years ago tomorrow..." There was the sound of a car door. "Hi Bob, yes I'm fine, just drive."

"Why do you remember the date Kitty?" her stepsister asked.

"If you did something that stupid you would remember too," there was a long pause. "It also was the day that Iraq invaded Kuwait." There was some murmuring. "All right, Bob. You got me. I'm that old." There was the muffled sound of laughter.

"How did you leave so fast, without him... without... without..." Patty was at a loss she was so shocked.

"On one hand, I transferred my commission from the Reserves to active duty and took the train up to the base, my old unit had drilled at—before I lost my nerve. On the other I couldn't face him so I said goodbye to ma and that was that.'"

"That was that?"

"You ask that like I had another plan?" Patty had chosen to be a housewife, but she knew it wasn't for everyone.

"Weren't you in school?" There was a sigh.

"Yeah, my third year of Rose Community, I was delivering pizzas. My boyfriend was from a rich family and was planning to marry me the summer after he finished his business degree. I could have finished school and become a PE teacher. But I wasn't into the schooling required to teach anything, even PE and I loved gym class.

"Wouldn't he have married you if you spent your life in the military?" Patty got up and looked at her wedding picture. Tony was a jolly obese Italian-American with a goatee on his chin and no hair on his head. During the pause his wife touched the picture, *thank God for you Te adoro mi amore.*

"I couldn't ask him to do that." There was the sound of finger tips patting a cellphone.

"Kitty, that's what marriage is. You don't need to ask. You just make sacrifices for each other. Did he love you enough to follow you from post to post?" The housewife was at the front window watching cars pass.

"That's the problem. He would have and I loved him too much to take him away from his dream. He had a life here. He had roots, a career, a church and now family..." Not that Russell Blaudel, since his dad's angina and retirement to Florida, wasn't good for the economy of Rose but what had they sacrificed?

"So you feel you did him a favor by loving him enough to let him go?" *Mull over that for a minute.*

"I...oh shit...you're twisting it all around." Kitty was flustered.

"So you shouldn't be afraid to face him, eh?" Patty put on her best Pierce Brosnan.

"I can't."

"Why not?"

"I don't know."

"Do you still love him?"

Chapter Eight
1989

"Does that feel better?" Russ was lying face down on a bench next to the track behind their old high school. His calf had gone out and Kitty had just stretched it out for him.

Slowly her boyfriend rolled over. Those smiling green eyes looked down at him. Those two worlds were enough to make anyone feel better. He began to sit up. They both wore shorts and sneakers. "What no happy ending Kit Kat?"

She gave him a playful dead arm, "shut up."

"Should I stand up?" She was more of an expert...of sorts—but she wasn't paying attention. "Kit Kat?"

"Come on my woose," she put her arm under his shoulder and he got up gingerly. It was tender. She took a step and he followed.

"It's tender." Russ studied her face.

"It will be," Kitty looked down, "Come on Hondo, walk it off." She led him by the hand to the track. "We'll walk one lap, slowly and then head for the car."

"You're the boss," her boyfriend agreed.

"You're going to be the CEO," his girlfriend laughed.

"I answer to you Kit Kat," she leaned around and kissed him closed mouth without missing a beat. "By the way, good John Wayne reference."

"Let's hope you're still saying that in twenty-five years," the athlete grinned.

"I plan to be saying that in fifty years," the future businessman argued. "Just keep boning up on John Wayne."

"That long?" Russ squeezed Kitty's hand.

"Always Kit Kat."

"Even though I'm a liberal jock," he laughed.

"Oh, you may be a bitch, but you're my bitch," she gave him a playful dead arm. "Ow hey!" She giggled and danced away. He didn't follow, walking the track his leg twinges.

"Shhh, woose." She giggled. "Is 'bitch' supposed to be a compliment?"

"'Well behaved women rarely make history,' you're never afraid to speak your mind even when you're wrong and I respect that," He grinned. "I wouldn't want to love a doormat."

"So being an outspoken bitch is a turn on?" they walked slowly together again.

"Why not?" she took his hand.

"That's probably why I fit with you so well.

Chapter Nine
2013

The phone rang. "Mom?" sitting in her daughter's apartment Sharon answered.

"Hello Kitty." A chuckle, "you here yet?" She wasn't mad. She knew she had pushed her daughter pretty hard.

"Ten minutes to the door. I'm sorry I hung up." Well, that was new.

"It's no big deal, really." There were boxes along one wall. The couch was nice, if not a boring shade of gray and the flat screen was hooked up. It was a two bedroom.

"Patty called." *Shit.*

"I'm sorry, Kitty, I swear, I didn't ask her." The mother stood, expecting to be asked to leave. One chair was littered with the things Sharon had bought.

"No, we had a great talk," somebody fell back on the couch.

"Really?" this was astounding.

"Monica had her call me," game, set and match for Mrs. Slater-Burns.

"Really? What did you speak of?" she played dumb.

"Ma, you know what we talked about. Russ Blaudel and what happened twenty-three years ago." *Gimme more kid.*

"And?"

"Tell me more about Russ Blaudel today." Her mother stood up and hopped up and down like Rocky, almost dropping the phone. "Mom," the phone was replaced, "Ma,"—but she heard her daughter giggling.

"He's not gay. He was terrified to come to my wedding and it was written all over his face why." That was honest and fair.

"What was written all over his face?"

"It was the same look he had every time I saw him. He never stopped loving *you.*" A mother knows. Worse fears? True.

"Right," the syllable was elongated. "What facts do we know?"

"Mona was a tramp," in her heart of hearts, Sharon always thought of Mona as Miss Not Kitty. This mother often wondered who was more heartbroken, she had loved Russ like a son and looked forward to,—

"I'm not one to criticize...easy virtue." There was a muffled laugh. "Shush Sergeant."

There was a muffled, 'yes ma'am,' over the phone.

"You weren't married at the time...times," they couldn't help but chuckle at the mom's slip. She may not approve, but she sometimes she laughed.

"Mother! I'm not that easy!" muffled laughing. "Shush Bob!"

"I know you daughter and know what you're like with men." Sharon crossed her legs and she wasn't sure—but she could swear she thought she heard the veteran scoff.

"I guess I do kind of make men squirm a little—shut up Bob!" There was more muffled laughing. "Maybe I tried hard to keep my bed full during the last twenty years, but that's because Russ wasn't in it. There was the sound of a hand hitting its own mouth. "Ow."

"Are you alright?" her mother got up.

"Yeah," her daughter agreed.

"I don't think there was room in his heart or in his bed for Mona, so even though he was kind to her, in the end heroically so, that woman sought her sexual release anywhere and everywhere else." Most of that was gossip. Sharon could do penance lady.

"Room?"

"I think you are there with him spiritually, always." Now that was opinion—then again his ghost followed her.

"But he took her back after she divorced him and left him?" Now that had surprised everyone. "He's a better man than I,—shut up Bob."

It was the parent's turn to laugh. "That was a three month convalescence when she was dying of cancer. That wasn't taking her back."

"He raised those kids alone, not even a regular maid or housekeeper?" There was some chatter. "We're parking."

"Oh good and yes—they are nothing like either one of you. Not athletes, not into business. They sang in high school and played instruments. If this old wife had to guess, I'd say they were twenty year old virgins."

"Really?"

"Yup." They both giggled. "He never missed a dance recital, play or debate. He was the most involved father of all my Sunday School kids."

"And does he live to his considerable means?" He hadn't been that materialistic in college but that's before his company exploded.

"Russ Blaudel?" Sharon laughed and there was a whirring sound in the phone. "He lives in the same house he lived in with his parents which I haven't seen any changes made to in two decades, though I hear Mona redid the kitchen. Russ drives a Chevy and buys suits at Walmart. There are lots of rumors that he gives away more than he spends, but I can't prove it."

"So, straight, chaste, cheap and square?" there was sarcasm in her voice.

"Better than that, he's fun to talk to and he has an ear and smile for anyone. He must sleep two hours a night." The mother fawned a little bit.

"Sounds like you like him," her daughter joked.

"Would've staying here and teaching PE been so terrible?" That was a terrible question.

"I honestly don't know." The door opened.

Chapter Ten
March 19th 1987

"Happy birthday Kit Kat." Smiling she opened the box.

It was a silver basketball on a silver chain. She flipped it over and on the back were four initials and a symbol. KS & RB. "Oh my God, Russ!"

"You're my jock and an athlete all the time, but you're also my girl all the time Kit Kat," she put her arms around him and kissed him.

"This is so beautiful," she immediately put it on. With the pixie cut there was no hair in the way. "I'll break my rule about no jewelry." She did up the clasp and pulled on the collar of her t-shirt to drop it between her breasts.

"Next to your heart Kit Kat?" she gave him a playful dead arm.

"Ow, Kit Kat!" he rubbed his arm.

"Shhh. Woose. Too sappy," she giggled.

She also calmed him. "Did I ever tell you how beautiful your eyes are," she clenched her first and then released it.

"You don't talk about my appearance that often," they stopped walking.

"You're not the kind of girl that needs to be flattered." She pushed him a bit.

"It doesn't mean I don't need to hear it sometimes," Kitty countered.

"I figure that there are women are beautiful and know it," she crinkled her nose, "bitches." That elicited a chuckle. "Women who are ugly and think they are beautiful."

"Idiots." They laughed.

"Women who are ugly and accept it," she shrugged. "Finally there are women who are beautiful and don't care."

"And you think that's me?" Kitty asked.

"Um, yeah," Russ explained.

"So I am beautiful?"

"If heaven were a face it would be yours, if joy were eyes," she gave him a playful dead arm. "Ow!" she laughed.

"A little thick." He frowned. Her eyes lit up. "But it makes me feel good."

"Yeah?"

"Yeah." She took his hand. "I guess you're better looking than...Arnold Stallone." They laughed together.

Chapter Eleven
August 2nd, 2013

Monica stood in Kitty's not inconsiderable bedroom at the ironing board working on a long skirt, one of the gifts. There was a bench at the foot of the bed where Patty sat crocheting and Sharon sat on the bed, legs crossed. Funny, considering the state of the room after only one day you'd never guess a retired colonel lived there.

The bathroom door was cracked and the woman of the house was bathing, invisible but audible. "How did she get in there alone?" Patty, wearing a lovely pink high cut blouse and black slacks, unfortunately she matched them with bright white nurse's shoes.

"Carefully," Sharon explained. She wore old lady cut white trousers, an ugly floral—in her defense it was a popular pattern for the septuagenarians and cream colored low heels. "Monica you really don't have to be doing this on your birthday."

"Oh please, I've been waiting ten years for her to talk to my dad," don't think the bathing veteran with the pixie cut couldn't hear everything through the door.

"I'm not going," Kitty called from the bathroom. "I'm staying home." Just because they couldn't see each other doesn't mean they couldn't argue.

"But it's your birthday," Patty argued to Monica maternally.

"Oh, dad took us out last night. Then Brett and I went to see *The Conjuring*. It was a good day." She grinned as she spoke. Her bracelet made a little noise.

"Was that any good?" Kitty called. "I love supernatural stuff."

"Oh it was great. Dad actually recommended it, he and Father Tom saw it last week." She moved the skirt.

"He's seeing R-rateds now?" the voice from the bathroom called.

"If they are soft Rs. He keeps saying he's not into those Arnold Stallone movies though." There were loud guffaws from behind the door.

"Arnold Stallone?" Sharon asked incredulously.

"He honestly doesn't know one from the other, at least he didn't thirty years ago. That's why when he picked a movie I got to watch endless hours of John Wayne." Monica giggled.

"Lucky you," mom turned the skirt over.

"Don't tell me he made you a fan of The Duke?" the veteran called.

"I kind of climbed on his lap when I was three and became a fan of old westerns on my own," the youngest woman in the room argued. "At first it was an excuse to cuddle with daddy, but it wasn't long until *Stagecoach* was my favorite movie."

"Stagecoach, really?" the veteran called.

"He has this old VHS,"—but she was cut off by an excited voice.

"Lucky you," came the response all too fast. "Wait a minute, I spoke too fast,"—

"You see Kitty," Monica retorted. "You need to go tonight."

"I'm not the same girl I was when I was your age." There was a bump in tub sound.

"Are you alright?" Sharon jumped. "Damn."

"Relax Ma! I'm fine!" The two younger women were taken aback for a moment. The elder woman took in stride. There was a silent spell. The iron was placed aside.

"I think you are exactly the same girl that you were twenty-three years ago in many ways Kitty." She crossed her arms as if to impress a jury.

"Grayer saggier and bitchier," laughter flowed from the bathroom.

"You left your dog tags on the night table along with a box from Walmart jewelry,"—she was obviously close.

"God damn it."

"What do we have here," Sharon turned on the bed to see and Patty got up.

"May I?" the future attorney held the box.

"No!" the colonel sounded like she was ordering troops.

"Yes," her mother argued, her face much closer to the inquisitor.

"All right," she opened it. "Simple silver chain and here on the dog tags I see a silver circle that is not military issue."

"Come on!" yelled Kitty from the bathroom.

"Relax daughter," her mother turned toward the bathroom. "They were right on the table. It's not like she's digging through drawers."

"Continue?" Patty was excited.

"Go head, read it," mom suggested.

"No-oh!" yelled the veteran.

"KS plus RB." Monica flipped it over. "Well, well," A silver basketball. "I know a man that thoughtful."

"Same man gave you that daddy's girl bracelet?" Sharon asked.

"That is a nice bracelet," Kitty agreed.

"Moving along," The iron off as she walked by. "You left your yearbook on top of these boxes."

"Shit."

"It wasn't there when I left last night, where you reminiscing last night daughter?" her mother pressed.

"Your yearbook is only well thumbed to one page. I can see that without opening it, do I need to bother?" the future attorney asked.

"No," there was movement in the bathroom. "You're going to make a good lawyer kid."

"I passed a basketball in your living room,"—

"Okay, I'm getting jealous. You're the anti-me. Everything I'd want in a daughter." Patty and Sharon looked at each other.

"And you're the mother I always wanted," that came out before Russ's daughter thought.

"You don't know me well enough to say that!" There was a long silence.

"The other day my brother and I tagged teamed dad about you for most of an hour, then he went to a meeting with Father Tom Hudson, Sharon says you went to high school with him as well," she looked to the eldest woman for confirmation, who nodded.

"We did." Kitty was chastened.

"My father, who is not a drinker, sat up staring at that damn yearbook and listening to *Same Auld Lang Syne* while getting drunk." She went and sat next to Sharon.

"*Same Auld Lang—shit*,"—Patty cut her off.

"*Syne*. It's by Dan Fogel,"—the veteran interrupted back.

"I know who sings it," the voice called back. "Son of a bitch, in a lot of ways he's still living in nineteen ninety."

"I know it," Russ's daughter agreed, "he did a great job raising me but he's dead inside."

"I had a damn good career in army...a damn good..." the veteran let her voice trail off, she couldn't bring herself to say 'life.'

"Where exactly were you serving during that last mission?" her stepsister asked.

"That's...classified." Then silence from behind the door.

"I'm the only one you've stayed in contact with since ninety, I don't remember you being happy, not like you were," her mother argued.

"I don't know. I thought I was making a difference." Then there was silence from the bathroom. They all waited. "I was defined."

"I know how dad felt back then," Monica argued. "Those were the days he was at his best. He loves you."

"Would staying and being a PE teacher have been horrible? Would you have been less happy?" Sharon asked.

"Wouldn't that have been making a difference?" Patty asked.

"I don't know." No one said a word about the Kit Kat wrapper taped to the yearbook or the fresh Kit Kat on the desk.

"Rose isn't that big Kitty. If you didn't come back to see dad, how can you expect to avoid him?" All three older women had to admit the college student was smart.

"I really don't know."

"So why did you come back?" the oldest woman in the room asked.

"I wanted out of Bethesda and the best therapist for my...condition is at the VA here. Also mom and Bill are here and Patty." Monica stood up.

"So what are you going to do when you run into him?" Silence. "Are you going to look away? Pretend you don't know him? You've both walked around for twenty-three years. In your uniform and his suit I'm sure you saved plenty of lives Kitty. Dad created two lives," she didn't mention the good his charities had done. "Well as near as I can see it, as the Duke said, 'you two may have been walking around, but it ain't livin.' Or something like that." She turned to the older two women. "If you'll excuse me, my phone's vibrating Brett's here."

She disappeared. Stunned to two older women didn't speak. "Spunky kid. I like her," came from the bathroom.

"She could've been yours," the step-sister spoke.

"She shoulda been yours," the mom agreed. "She still can be yours."

"I blew my shot when I disappeared in the night." Her mother stood.

"Can you honestly tell me you wouldn't have been happier as a PE teacher married to Russ?" Nothing. "Come on."

"Put the skirt on Kitty," Patty argued, "at least try."

Chapter Twelve
August 2nd, 1990

Russ sat at the train station. He had missed her. Ironically, Dan Fogelberg came on the radio.

We drank a toast to innocence. We drank a toast to time. Reliving, in our eloquence Another Auld Lang Syne...

Not thirty miles away Kitty sat on a cold and lonely train, surrounded by people. She put headphones in. *Frigan radio.* Dan Fogelberg was on that same station.

Eight years to the day later on August 2nd, 1998 Kitty sat outside her barracks in Fort Bliss, Texas listening to the radio when she was off duty. Not too far Russ away was in Dallas on business in a taxi on the way to Dallas Fort Worth airport after a meeting. Coincidentally they were listening to the same station.

Lieutenant Slater's and Mr. Blaudel's blood ran cold independently of each other's.

She said she's married her an architect. Who kept her warm and safe and dry. She would have liked to say she loved the man But she didn't like to lie

"You coming?" Captain Johnson touched Kitty's shoulder and she was brought back from the moment.

In Dallas a very archaic pager beeped. It was Mona. "I'll call her from the airport, probably about the kids," and Russ forgot about the song.

Part Three

Chapter One
August 2nd, 2013

The DJ was loud and two people were late, mentally, physically, literally and spiritually. It was eighties music for an eighties crowd. Russ heard the music as he waited in line and then Regina Cleary signed him into the damn reunion. Regina had been the Valedictorian—and chairwoman, yes chairwoman, of the yearbook committee. "Oh it's you." She turned her nose up at his name. "You're the one who is always in church." Yes there are people who still speak to us that way.

"Freedom of religion Gina," he signed his name and she scribbled it on a sticker for him to wear. Rusty had driven him and Monica had picked out a suit, that's how much mixing in they did.

"Well you know that the founding fathers *and* mothers..." ignoring her, the businessman looked around the gym and two hundred people, most of whom were not etched into his memory. Some danced, some congregated around the punch bowl and most talked. There were a lot of women built like 43 and dressed like 18. That was enough to cringe. One wall had a banner welcoming them back the other wall had blow-ups of yearbook pictures. None of note.

Then the wiry father of twins saw something across the way at a part of the gym not used for the party. There were two other nearby halls with bathrooms and several other exits, this one was ignored. Everything went quiet.

"I guess," Russ agreed noncommittally. He was not listening. Over Regina's shoulder he saw a seated silhouette out the doors to the darkened vestibule. It held trophies and unused older bathrooms. The locked exterior doors faced Saint M's across Basilica Street. The left side on the way out had the trophies, the right side was photos and a wall of fame. One photo was Kitty holding a trophy. "Excuse me."

The seated figure was in a familiar spot.

Chapter Two
1986

Long after the final buzzer and a loss the game's big scorer stood in the doorway of the gymnasium looking through the vestibule out the doors' windows at passing cars. A sweat stained basketball shirt, baggy shorts. Toned legs, her boyfriend put his hand on her shoulder. "Kit Kat."

Kitty put her hand on his. "Was I good?" she asked.

"Good enough to win." She started to turn to him. There were tears in her eyes.

67-66. Three point shot at the buzzer. The Rose Thorns took them down, despite her 50 point effort. "I lost."

"Hey, you played a hell of a game," despite her pixie cut her chestnut bangs were matted to her head. "It's not your fault...a team played, a team lost. Never let them see you bleed trooper." He squeezed her shoulder and she embraced him.

Damn it Russ, you always knew how to make me feel better.

"I love you egghead." They separated.

"I love you too jock." He took her hand.

"I think I want to get out of here." Her mom was working. His parents weren't there. They were seniors in high school.

"Do you want to change?" she shook her head.

"Take me to your home, I can change there." That was true but more dangerous for him.

They went out the doors and around the corner walking hand in hand silently. She knew he had walked to school and there were probably clothes in his closet that were hers. They were joined at the hip after all.

Chapter Three
2013

"I'm sorry. I thought I could face you." The figure was in a wheelchair. The left side of her face and her left eye was bandaged. Her chestnut pixie cut was graying but all there.

"Twenty-three years is a long time," Russell James Blaudel leaned against the next doorway and put his hands in his suit pockets.

"I never even said good bye." The seated figure pushed her switch and the chair rolled into the darkness.

"Time wounds all heals," he made a face at his malapropism. "Or something like that Kit Kat." How odd it was to say her name after so long.

"Are you smiling?" Colonel Kathleen Marie Slater, U.S. Army—retired looked.

Whirled her chair to face him. Yeah—she could still kick his ass. She wore a long black skirt that almost covered the casts and black flats. Her turtleneck sweater was teal and lovely.

"No uniform?" She shook her head.

"Mom talked me out of it." Kitty looked at Russ, "you seem calm."

"Do you expect me to rage? If you think I could be angry with your, or curse your name then you never knew me." Russ turned to go. "Goodbye Kit Kat." It was barely a whisper.

"Wait Blaudel, please." Her voice cracked. That made him pause.

"Here's your chance." He waited.

"That's not why I'm here." The music picked up again. "Fuck they're loud."

That made him laugh and he turned to her. "Colonel Slater, Silver Star, Distinguished Service Cross, Legion of Merit and three purple hearts—."

"Four," she was still correcting him.

"Four." He sat next to her on the stairs, messing up the suit his daughter had picked out to make him look 'old time movie star dapper.' There was a pause. "Those and about two dozen more medals and you're hesitating."

"I,"—

"Come on Kit Kat, its D-Day." Okay, they weren't that old.

99

"Well, one third of America's Greatest Generation hesitated Business Major," she finally grinned and wiped her free eye, which was the same eye that haunted his dreams.

"What do you want Colonel?"

"Please don't call me that!" She barked. A couple people at the punch bowl looked at them and then went back to what they were doing.

He raised a hand. "I'm sorry." There was long hesitation.

"Um," the veteran of three 'wars,' looked at her lap. "What you said."

It had been barely audible over the music. "What?"

"I'm...I was wrong." That made Russ study the face he had memorized so long ago.

"Kitty, what are you saying?" The music changed.

They recognized it. They looked at the gymnasium. He had gotten drunk to this song the a couple times after she left. *Same Auld Lang Syne.*

"Can I buy you a cup of coffee?"

They looked at the new wooden ramp up one side of the stairs to the doors that didn't need a key on this side. "Um...yeah."

Chapter Four
1986

"Okay, but I have to be back for practice." In jeans and hooded sweatshirts with big M's on them two teenagers started down Basilica Way to Dunkin' Donuts.

"Do I ever make you late Kit Kat?" the pixie haired athlete pecked her egghead on the cheek.

"Often." They giggled.

"Do we have to go all the way to Dunkin'?" They turned down Fifth Street, houses on the right with them, park on the left.

"It's warm enough, do you want to stop at the bench and make fun of dog walkers." Russ just laughed and put his arm around her.

"Can I tell you something awkward?" Kitty studied her young man's face.

"You're nervous Blaudel." She pulled away and gave him a playful dead arm. He started to protest and she laughed harder. "Shhh. Woose."

"Kitty," then he just said it. "I love you."

That caused a pause and an athlete studied her egghead's face. "Good," was the slow response then no movement at all for a moment. "Because I love you too."

Then Russ was kissed full on by Kitty and if had been a movie someone's foot would have popped.

They separated and hesitated. "Um....bench?

"Um...Yeah." They walked in silence. Then they sat. "Kitty, there was one other girl said that to me."

She raised an eyebrow. "Oh really?"

"Brittany told me she loved me," there was a long paused. "Shit I loved her like a little sister and I knew...well...it was a good memory for her to take with her."

I'm going to die Russ.

No, Tiny, you're going live.

I'm nine, not stupid.

Well, you have to live.

Why? You're already taken.

Oh Brittany, you get better and I'll marry you.

Heh. I love you.

I love you too kid.

"I knew that. She adored you." Nine months to that day was when Kitty's little sister Brittany had died from Leukemia. She had a crush, he had made the child smile.

"I have a present for you." He pulled a wrapped rectangle from the pocket of his hoody.

"Sappy?" He nodded. "Remember that day, about a year and a half ago, when she rallied and your mom let us take her on a hike at the state park...as long as we made her rest at every bench," about 150 feet.

Not so long ago. "One year ago today." He corrected her. She opened the box. There was a pressed flower—they didn't know the breed—framed with the date of the hike.

"Is this the flower you picked for her?" One purple-pink flower in an ocean of green and brown off the trail and one very nice teenage boy had walked through a whole lot of tall grass.

"You're mom saved it."

"I love it." Kitty buried her head in Russ's chest. "Thank you."

"She was family to me too." That's how he felt.

She embraced him "I don't ever want there be a time when you and me aren't me and you Kit Kat." She squeezed him tighter.

"Was that a proposal?" they eyed each other. Hers danced.

"Was there ever a doubt?"

Chapter Five
2013

"You know, you look fine," Russ mumbled.

Kitty gave him the death stare. "I look like Nick Fury." A pause. "Having a tank land on you will do that."

"Actually I was thinking you look more like Mystique." She raised an eyebrow.

"And?" They kept walking and rolling.

"The whole couldn't face me thing." The eyebrow went back up.

"Fuck you Blaudel." That took him aback. "I don't give a rat's ass about my injuries."

"Neither do I!" Some things never change. "You still got a great temper."

"I couldn't face you because of what happened twenty-three years ago." The businessman sighed. "I was too scared to say goodbye."

"My Rick Blaine in the rain moment." Kitty just gave him a look rolling down Fifth Street.

"I didn't send you a handwritten letter and you don't have a sidekick that plays the piano." They looked at the bench facing the park.

"No, but I have a friend named Sam who sings...karaoke." That made the veteran laugh.

"Sam is still singing in public?" Just a nod. "Good old Sam."

"Gay." They looked at each other and shrugged.

"Sit?"

He did. She looked at the view. "No dogs tonight."

"As I recall there were plenty of nights we sat here with nothing to look at," Russ loosened his tie. Too many.

"I always had something to look at, he waited, "still do." Even as he said it the businessman shifted on the bench, as she parked next to it.

"I will walk again," nothing. "I have casts on under this skirt, mom's idea to look more girly." She didn't tell him his daughter had helped. He shrugged. "I never had to look more girly for you, I was always a girl when you saw me."

"Well, eventually you were a woman." He looked at his own shoes.

"We had some fun on this bench, as I recall," Kitty ran her hand along the handle. "Wait a minute!" It seemed odd to her.

"Same spot, same view—different bench. I guess they replaced that old wooden deal about ten years ago."

"So much has changed." The veteran scratched at something under the bandage.

"More is the same. I have the same address, Blaudel Inc. has the same address. Same church I went to with you. My kids went to that high school. Same park. Same city. Hell, the mayor has the same last name."

She rolled her eye. He still loved that. "Lenny Fox...ugh." Their class clown.

"That's Lenard Fox junior Esquire." Russ laughed. "I didn't vote for him." His father had been mayor twenty-five years before.

"Neither did I." They forced a chuckle and then were silent. "I guess many things are the same a lot sometimes."

After a pause he corrected her grammar, hell he tutored her in English and Math back in the eighties. "In many ways." There was a hesitation.

"What?"

"You said 'same a lot,' you meant 'the same in many ways,' it's better English." Kitty gave him a playful dead arm.

"Hey," he rubbed his arm.

"Shhh. Woose." Still felt good. Too good.

They did shush. They looked at the empty park. After a couple minutes Russ asked the inevitable. "What do you want Kit Kat?"

"Um, if I was one hundred percent honest you'd ... shit, well...let me try say this right." He waited. "I'm Sorry."

"You said that already."

"No, I mean I'm sorry you thought that I believed I was choosing the better—I mean... FUCK. I'm saying everything wrong...I was..." the colonel let her voice trail off.

"Look, I'll make it easy for you. I forgave you in ninety. I left in the past. You walked the path you had to walk and I walked mine. Yes, I married the wrong woman, but I had—have two great kids. I have a good leisurely management style at the company. I'm active at Saint M's. I'm happy. I'm sorry the army's over, I truly am but you are forgiven." Russ got up. "Good luck Kit Kat," and just like that he started to walk away.

It was an early Fall apparently. Leaves began to fall. The irony was not lost on Kitty as he walked away.

"Russell Blaudel!" That made him feel small. She was a master at that. He stopped walking. She still owned him.

Chapter Six
1986

"Just relax Russ. You need to learn." They were on his parents back lawn, shorts, t-shirts and barefoot.

"I'm about one-sixty five. I won't be doing much fighting." It didn't happen often but his little pixie haired angel's cute lips curled into a sneer.

"Russell Blaudel!" That made him feel small. "I'm a hundred and one pounds and I'll knock you on your ass."

"I'm not gonna hit you Kit Kat." She crossed her arms.

"Fine, just try and stop me." Then without warning she took his wrist and flipped him on his ass. Looking down at him his beloved looked like an elf grinning impishly. "Use your opponent's weight against him."

She helped him up. "Right." She flipped him again. "Weight against him." Laughing, Kitty helped him up again.

"What happens when Sam Culley takes a swing at me," now Sam was their buddy and that was unlikely, but he was two ten of muscle.

"Avoid the punch, don't block it." She pecked him on the cheek.

"Okay, show me slowly," Russ grinned.

Chapter Seven
2013

Russ looked at the visible portion of her beautiful face. Still all he dreamed of—just all woman.—that thought was dispelled quickly. "What else is there?"

"I was wrong. The army was not the better part." Now she tells him. "It didn't really define me. I didn't know for sure until I saw you."

"And?"

"I figured that out in Kuwait." He sat.

"That would have been the time for a letter Kit Kat." She looked away. "What do want?" Russ asked. She couldn't get the words out. "Damn it Kathleen!"

"Wha,"—that was the first time he had ever yelled at her—or used her full name.

"I'm out of patience," he whispered. "What,"—

"Same thing I wanted when we were ten, or sixteen, or nineteen—or in in Kuwait—or the DMZ, or Afghanistan or Iraq or at twenty, thirty, forty or lying with a tank on top of me thinking I was going to die without admitting it." The broken bones ached.

"What's that?" His heart ached but his anger flared hotter. He did sit next to her electric wheelchair again.

"If you have to ask that then you never knew me." Russ rubbed his hands together between his knees and looked at the ground.

"Well, I guess we really were strangers." Neither believed that, but you say things when you're angry. He had been building this mad a long time.

"I don't think so." Kitty wheeled in front of him and slowly gingerly ran her fingers through his hair, the way she had done twenty-five years before. "I just realized we want the same thing. You kids seem to think so, as does my mom."

"What?" Blaudel was hardened.

"You see my mom has kept tabs on all of you." *Oh, Okay, here it is!*

"And?" he leaned back, but looked at her.

"You're dad refused to take military contracts, but your company did several billion with Uncle Sam last year. Non-weapon, all military."

"And?" they were good investments.

"That's not nothing." She wasn't stupid.

"It's business." Yes, but not *just* business.

"I know for a fact—and no I'm not proud of how I know—that you undersold all competitors by a lot—and your company innovated body armor, boots, helmets and transports." He shrugged.

"Those helmets paid for my Chevy," he was being crass, you really had to piss Russ off to for him to be crass.

"One of your helmets saved my life you son of a bitch."

A single tear went down the businessman's face. "Kit Kat,"—

"Saint M's hospital has been given enough money by an anonymous donor in the last five years to build a Children's Cancer wing that looks like a castle. They have a grant to pay for one child's bills per year." This time Russ kept his mouth shut. "Do I need to break in, or do you want to tell me that you're doing that in Brittany's memory."

It took a minute. "Yes," he whispered.

"My mom was going to lose the house fifteen years ago. Times were hard, she had lost her job. She hadn't gotten the one where she met Bill yet. The day you became president of Blaudel Inc., which has stock in the bank they refinanced her, coincidence?"

Russ couldn't talk. His tears fell like rain.

"I won't pretend I was a saint. I decided in boot camp I couldn't come back because what I did to you was unforgivable. I couldn't even face you then. If...anyway, I went to WestPoint." Not news. "I was a little slut there. I couldn't come home, I had ruined the only love I'd ever know," Kitty went on. "So I ruined *me*."

"Kit Kat,"—she put a finger to his lips.

"Please let me finish." She took her hand away. "Sex was my drug. It masked the pain. I'd close my eyes and pretend whoever he was—he was you." She wiped a tear.

"Do you think it matters one man or a million or how many men, or women," she grinned, just for a moment, "you've been with."

"No." Not to him. There was no judgement in Blaudel. Just pain.

"It's not part of us. This conversation is about you and me." That surprised Kitty.

"You don't want to know?" Russ shook his head.

"I never asked Mona either—and that affected an us." He shrugged. "She and I were an us. You and me aren't an us and weren't an us when you did it. We haven't been an us for a long time."

"Oh." Kitty leaned back dejected. A dog walker—leisure suited yuppy man—ignored them.

"I'd sit in church and ask God how I could have loved you better to make you stay. Then, well,"—he shrugged.—"I figured you loved the army more."

"You were wrong about that." A nod. "By the time mom's house was saved and I realized you still loved me you were married to a woman who didn't love you."

Russ gave Kitty his handkerchief and then used his tie to blow his own nose before taking it off. "We all make mistakes." He then put the soiled garment in his pocket.

"The kids,"—-

"He looks exactly like me at twenty and their twins." She waited, rolling her eye. "And their amazing."

"So I did something fifteen years ago I hadn't done since I left."

"Pray a novena?" They laughed.

"Captain Selleck, good egg, if he wasn't a priest I may have—anyway, he was our company chaplain. I went to Confession and told him our story. Then I took his bible,"—

"Breviary." She gave him a dead arm. "Hey."

"Actually, I deserved that one. He corrected me too, even gave me a bible that I never read." A pattern. "But I swore on that breviary that no matter what I was fighting for you." No one asked her to.

"You what!" Somehow, in a misguided way, she felt that she was his champion.

"Russ, don't you get it, everyone fights for something."—This was new.

"Courtly love," funny that's not all he dreamed of.

"Maybe." He had certainly kept home fires burning.

"Maybe not."

"Everybody who fights, fights for something. Loyalty, money, flag, hate or love...maybe others. I was fighting for *your* freedom right up until I flipped that tank." Screaming his name.

"Kit Kat. I want to believe you, but she's been gone a decade. You could have written...called?" his face filled with angry. Her lips had been loosed by his face.

"I was scared. I still am. I wouldn't be here now if I wasn't retired...that doesn't change how I feel." She wiped her eye. "I could...should...I...your..."

"That I'm your second choice in life?" He raged on. He couldn't...he couldn't even form the thought about what he couldn't do.

"*We* have a second chance."

He didn't have an answer for that.

Chapter Eight
2008

Fox News was interviewing an American Lieutenant Colonel about a foul up. Her name was Slater and the viewer was glued to the television. The phone rang. "Captain Michaels is suffering from exhaustion."

"Hello," Russ Blaudel answered the house phone. It never rang at night unless something was bad. It was.

"Daddy, I need your help." He stood up.

"What's wrong Monica?" She was supposed to be at a safe party with her friend Dani, whose parents were supposed to be there.

"There's alcohol here dad, I don't know where Dani's parents are, I'm hiding in her bedroom. And daddy, there's college boys here." Thank God it was a portable phone because he was already at the door.

"Will there be charges against Captain Michaels?" he ignored the TV.

"Where's your cellphone Monica?" she wasn't the caller ID.

Monica hesitated. "I dropped it a beer." Everyone makes mistakes.

"Relax and stay where you are, I'm on my way." He made the seven minute drive in three. The house was nice but not posh. There at least fifteen males and females between fifteen and twenty-one on the front lawn. Russ parked on the street.

He wore loafers, button down, suit jacket and khakis. The door was open. Dani was sitting on the front step crying. "My parents will kill me," the sixteen year old sobbed with the bedlam going on around her. Togas, kegs. Teenage girls and college men kissing and one kid was tossing ping pong balls against the TV, which ironically was on Fox News.

"Of course the army does not approve of Captain Michael's actions," Kitty went on. *Oh Kit Kat help me.*

"Look, I see nothing and I won't tell your parents. I just came for my daughter," *thank God Rusty went to see a movie with Lenny's kid.*

"My room, second door on left," the teen pointed up the stairs and up Russ went.

There was a scream and he kicked the door open. His daughter, wearing a much lower cut top and shorter skirt than she had left the house with was doing her best to avoid a large football player. "Come on Monica."

"Hey frat boy," the businessman said calmly.

"Get your own room old man," the kid was drunk, not just an asshole.

"That's my daughter who turns sixteen next week." Russ took a step.

"Oh, well, fuck you then." That was enough.

"Look, there are plenty of legal girls downstairs, who, I'm sorry to say, are all up for it kid, you'll just have to pass, high school." The goon was doing a gorilla impersonation.

"Asshole I'm a sophomore at URose." Oh. Eighteen or nineteen. Probably 220. *What had*

Kit Kat sad?

"Old fart," the football player lunged for the Monica's dad and he side stepped. The big oaf went face first into the door jam. "Shit." He turned, swung and missed.

'Then when he's off balance get him with a right cross,' Kit Kat's voice played like an MP3 player in his head.

So Russ took down the football player with one swing.

"Daddy?" Monica asked.

"I dated a soldier once." He draped his suit jacket over her shoulders. "Let's get out of here before King Kong wakes up."

"I'm so dead," he put his arm around his princess.

"Relax." He led her down the stairs.

"Good night Dani," Monica coughed.

"I'd call the cops Dani," The dad led his daughter to his car and drove away. "Breath, are you alright Monica?"

"Dad, that was amazing," he shrugged.

"She taught me well." *Kit Kat you're my hero.*

"How much trouble am I in?" The teenager was shivering.

"None." He pulled away.

"What?" his daughter couldn't believe it.

"We had a deal, I would trust you to make good choices as long as you would call me if you found yourself at a drinking party or without a safe ride. You kept your end of the bargain." Monica smiled. That had been the deal.

"Thank you Daddy." She took his hand.

"But next time you say 'Dani's house' I want to call her parents."

"Fair enough." Her makeup was ruined. She had grown up half way to beautiful but she'd always be his little girl.

"Dunkin Donuts drive through?" Monica's dad always knew what to say.

"Yes..." she was still nervous.

"What?" as he drove away.

"Who was the soldier?" Sooner or later Monica was going to ask questions.

Russ sighed. "Her name was Kathleen Slater, we dated in high school and the first part of college and her a reservist."

"Was she pretty?" he sighed again.

"Aye lass," came a faux Scottish accent. "She was fair. Athletic and tough, with soft green eyes and chestnut hair, always in a pixie cut.

"Your fawning dad," he blushed.

"You don't need to hear this daughter," she giggled.

"Your next wife?" he grimaced and turned into Dunkin' Donuts.

"Quit it or I won't get you your latte." They laughed.

"You're a hero dad but a little too much John Wayne and not enough Superman." Ignoring the statement Russ put the radio on. They had to grin.

Where have all the cowboys gone?

Chapter Nine
2013

"There is one piece missing," Kitty went on.

"Shoot." *What the hell?*

"Well, probably a few. But tell me this, do you have contacts in the military from your contracts that owe you favors?" Russ shrugged. "Humor me."

The businessman let out a long sigh. "Kit Kat,"—

"Please, for old time sake," he wiped his hands down his face.

"All right. In descending order of rank; General Jack Celano, General Ben Peck, General Lianna Olson, Colonel Megan Brewster, Colonel B.J. Mikkelsen, Colonel Mark Olschan, Lieutenant Colonel Sarah Rogers, Major Valerie Danson and Major Sheldon Levine."

"So if you called,"—puppet master much?

"Kit Kat, I'll level with you. Every prototype, the shoes, the armor, the helmet," he touched her wounded check as gently as he'd hold a baby's head, "I held every one and thought of you wearing it, I never told anyone at work or my kids, but it was all for you." The hand dropped." Even the year Mona and I actually shared a bed and then the last two decades alone, of course the years before, I fell asleep praying for you and woke up thinking of you. But I never made a call on your behalf or tried to interfere in your life, I knew you'd get those eagles on your own. Without the accident it'd be four stars"

Kitty giggled, for real this time. "Just one star. I don't need an act of Congress." More than one star requires an act of Congress.

"Peck and Celano would still outrank you." She shrugged.

"Olson....Whoa, Brewster, Celano and Danson?" His head fell and the veteran chuckled. "Son of a bitch. You are my hero."

"No," Russ looked up. "Don't say that." He pointed to her legs and to her eye and then he picked up her callused hands, her confirmed killers, and kissed them. "You are my hero, you were always my hero."

"Shut up." She gave him a playful dead arm. "And you aren't a woose. I heard about a frat boy who was arrested four years ago crying that you kicked his ass." The businessman shrugged. "Of course he made you out to be six six and three hundred."

117

"You shut up." Remember that frightening night he shut her down.

"Let me tell you what a hero is. A hero is a man who raises two kids almost by himself when their mother abandons them. A hero is the man who nursed his ex-wife through cancer and paid the bills. A hero is a man that rescued his daughter from a drunk football player. A hero is a teenager boy who walked fifty feet in waist high grass to pick a flower"-

Blaudel changed the subject. "The VA will take care of you, their combat related." He shrugged. "Like you said, you'll walk again."

"The eye won't heel. The other tank operator is dead." He took her hand.

"Could you have avoided it?" Kitty looked away.

"I should have." Yes she should have, or so she thought.

Russ frowned. "That's not what I asked."

"A hundred tank commanders, seventy of them have a fifty fifty shot." Tears welled again.

"Then let it go." She looked at him and nodded. He waited. "That's it. You had a better man than me the last twenty-three years," Russ explained.

"I assure you that none of the men," she grimaced at the number, "were better men."

"Uncle Sam. You had the country." Our heroine looked at our hero with disbelief.

"What?"

"Oh come on, you'd still be in the army. You always dreamed of being General Kathleen Slater. Lianna told me that you'd have made it by fifty, hell you'd have had it by forty, but she said you...make too many waves...and when a woman says that about a woman..."

"Oh my God." She turned the chair and wheeled it away.

"Kit,"—better to get it out.

"Don't you dare call me that," she was crying.

"What do you mean?" Russ hopped up and chased her.

"You heard *nothing*." Now she was pissed.

"I heard everything, but I can't undo twenty-three years." She had to give him that.

Kitty turned the chair around. "All my life..."

"All your life?" That was a statement he wanted to hear the end of.

"All my life I wanted to be Kathleen Blaudel. I know we made each other better people and we can better people together than we've been apart." Two decades of bad choices.

Chapter Ten
August 2, 1990

Russ went a jewelry store on Connecticut Avenue. He didn't see Kitty's Volkswagen drive by and turn into the dealership. Nor did he see the Taxi pick her up when she sold it. His back was to the window.

The saleswoman was good looking. The word Cougar hadn't really been coined yet but for a twenty-year old buying his girlfriend a ring a woman in her forties with a low cut blouse and a starry necklace showing the girls off compliment by a tight miniskirt, also black was what his son would someday call a cougar. The name tag read Bernice, funny what you remember.

"What can I get you?" she was a saleswoman who used flirtation and it worked.

"I need a diamond," she raised her eyebrows. "For my girlfriend."

Bernice nodded. Then she waited. "Ring?"

Russ blinked. "Yes, yes. An Engagement ring." He was nervous.

"Okay," another pause. "size?"

"Oh," he tried so hard not to look at the Cs in front of him. "My pinky."

"Sir?"

"My pinky and her finger are the same size." She sized him. It made him uncomfortable.

"Here are our most popular." He saw a price tag.

"Okay, Bernice, maybe if I tell you my budget." So he did. His dad hadn't started paying him full time yet—just allowance until he graduated.

"All right, look at these." Thank God they were slow and the other clerk went in the back.

"May I see that one?" Small, cute. Just like Kitty.

"Well,"—Bernice seemed doubtful.

"I'll pay cash." He did.

"Let's see here." It didn't have to be sized.

"It's fate." He put it in his breast pocket and was about to leave when the other salesman ran out front. He was aghast.

"Marvin?" Bernice asked.

"Iraq has invaded Kiwi." Yeah, that's what we knew. He got the country wrong.

"I think you mean Kuwait," Kit Kat's egghead corrected.

"Know it all," Marvin chided.

Russ didn't wait. He was out the door. He went to his Bonneville and drove to Kitty's. Sharon answered the door. "Hey Russ." She looked sad.

"Are you alright Sharon?" her face fell further.

"She didn't tell you?" the mother asked.

The ring was burning a hole in his pocket. "Who tell me what?"

"Are you sure miss Slater?" The captain on the bus asked. Her name tag read 'Olson.'

"Yes," she got on the bus. *Before I lose my nerve.*

The radio was on.

"You'll be good," Olson said. "You're a tough one, I can see that.

"Are you career?" she asked.

"Supplier to the rank and file." The captain was laughing.

"Sounds important," Kitty spoke blankly.

"What's his name?" Lianna asked.

"Russ,—how'd you know?" The older woman had her read.

"It's obvious. Did you break his heart or did he break yours?" the older woman asked.

"I crushed his, I left without a trace," *didn't I?*

"Well, if he loves you, he'll forgive you,"—a voice called from the front.

"Excuse me," the captain rushed to the front.

More news on Kuwait and a speech from the president.

Chapter Eleven
2013

"What Day?"

Russ reached under his t-shirt and grabbed his silver chain he'd warn since his Confirmation. Then he tore it off. "The day I bought this."

"You were fourteen when you got that crucifix,"—he held the ring up and pocketed the rest of the necklace.

"I bought it while you were leaving." He squeezed it in his hand. "From that day I have worn it." They stood there. "If I could trust you to stay faithful I'd put it on you right now. But I can't." He tossed in it the bushes and walked away.

"How can you say that?" the tears were soaking her bandages. She rolled after him. He turned angrily and spat his truth. Several windows opened at the shouting on the suburban street.

"I've loved you since I was ten years old," oh the mouse was roaring now. "The day I bought that ring my childhood ended. We've both lived lives—whole lifetimes...we aren't those stupid kids anymore." The early fall leaves were falling. Russ kept walking away.

This time he was leaving.

She felt that old familiar pain he had felt when he saw her sitting there at the gym.

The pain he had felt when he had heard that she had left.

This can't be the end.

He was walking out of her life.

Chapter Twelve
September 3rd, 1975

A little boy with black hair sat reading Doctor Seuss on a wooden bench next to the playground. He ignored the other children squealing with glee. He was not a fat kid, just not a budding young athlete like the little chestnut haired girl that walked up to him.

"Aren't you going to play today?" Russell Blaudel looked up at a cute little girl. He'd always known her name. He couldn't remember actually meeting her, but that day on the playground during kindergarten was where their story began for him.

"Why?" he asked Kathleen Slater. He wore plaid shorts and a white polo. She wore white shorts and red t shirt. They both wore sneakers. Ah, the seventies.

"It's fun. You can't read all the time." The boy grinned as Kitty laughed at him.

"You like the jungle gym?" she kept laughing at him and tagged his shoulder. She liked all sporty things. It was the way she was. He liked books. It was the way he was.

"You're it," she turned and ran away from him to the monkey bars.

Well, he couldn't let it end there.

Russell James Blaudel put the book down and followed her.

Chapter Thirteen
2013

This time Kitty followed.

"*You* aren't walking out of *my* life. That's a mistake *I* make. You're too smart and you feel too much," Kitty finally spoke at the corner. There was the Dunkin' Donuts.

Anger spent and tears dried up. Russ walked up the sidewalk depression to the door and opened it. She kept wheeling after him. "You want that cup of coffee?" He gestured for her to come in.

Now Kit Kat grinned. She followed.

Fin

About the Publisher

Accepting manuscripts in the most categories. We love to help people get their words available to the world.

Revival Waves of Glory focus is to provide more options to be published. We do traditional paperbacks, hardcovers, audio books and ebooks all over the world. A traditional royalty-based publisher that offers self-publishing options, Revival Waves provides a very author friendly and transparent publishing process, with President Bill Vincent involved in the full process of your book. Send us your manuscript and we will contact you as soon as possible.

Contact: Bill Vincent at rwgpublishing@yahoo.com

Milton Keynes UK
Ingram Content Group UK Ltd.
UKHW011949160224
437951UK00001B/129

9 798869 163080